W9-AUD-869

THE LUCK OF THE IRISH

THE LUCK OF THE IRISH

✦ ✦ ✦

OUR LIFE IN COUNTY CLARE

by
Niall Williams
and Christine Breen

Published by
Soho Press, Inc.
853 Broadway
New York, N.Y. 10003

Library of Congress Cataloging-in-Publication Data

Williams. Niall. 1958–
The luck of the Irish : our life in County Clare / by Niall
Williams and Christine Breen.
p.   cm.
ISBN 1-56947-022-7
1. Clare (Ireland)—Social life and customs.   2. William, Niall,
1958–   —Homes and haunts—Ireland—Clare.   3. Breen, Christine,
1954–   —Homes and haunts—Ireland—Clare.   4. Farm life—Ireland—
Clare. I. Breen, Christine. 1954–   . II. Title.
DA990.C59W549   1955
941.9'3—dc20   94-26199
                                                                              CIP
Book design and composition by The Sarabande Press
Manufactured in the United States of America

10 9 8 7 6 5 4 3 2 1

For Joseph and Deirdre
Lubaloo

The Luck of
The Irish

✦ ONE ✦

A damp day in November. I am cycling the three miles of curving road into the village of Kilmihil to begin my day's teaching. Flecks of yellow blossom are on the gorse bushes, not as abundant as in springtime, but in this, their second blooming, a bright welcome. The winter has been easy on us so far and the rolling landscape I pedal through seems suspended in a faded green. It will be a long drizzling time before the color in the fields deepens, the hay rises in the meadows, and the tractors thrum through the summertime. Now the countryside lies pale and dripping in soggy tranquility. A car coming and going along the rising and falling gray thread of the village road serves as brief punctuation, exaggerating the stillness in the moment after it has gone over the hill and silence falls between the hedgerows again.

Behind me, almost a mile across the lumpy green handkerchief of the Hayes' farm, I can see our house in the little copse of fir trees, a low white cottage with smoke from the morning's fire suspended like a plume in the windless day. The green hill of Upper Tumper rising behind it and the valley spread before it, there it is, Kiltumper Cottage, our home in Clare. It is the place we had *come* to, the place Chris's grandfather had left almost a century before to find a life in America, and now the place that has been our home for nearly ten years. Cycling across the serenity of the morning, I looked back as I always did to see the chimney smoke. There is something comforting in that home fire slowly burning. And I thought, briefly, of the life in New York that might have been ours, a life full of contrasts with the one we lead now.

A day here is marked by simple details: I, on my bicycle, greeted as "sir" by the children I pass on my way to the village secondary school; Chris in the kitchen, our toddler, Joseph, at her heels, as she packs lunch for our daughter, Deirdre, before driving her a mile and a half "out the country" to Clonigulane, the century-old two-room two-teacher schoolhouse; the solitary road, cattle nosing along the ditches, their breaths hawing up over the old strands of rusting barbed wire that barely enclose them. Blackthorn and whitethorn, gorse, bare fuchsia, berried with pale dewdrops and hung with glistening webs; loops of briar falling out shoulder high onto the road; bits of things, plastic bags, sticks, baler twine blown away and tangled and wet in dungy puddles; branches cut to block gaps and freed by night winds, leaving muddy plashed places where the cattle broke out and wandered a hundred yards or so, eating the grass in the roadside ditches. A tractor in the distance loaded with round black-wrapped bales of silage. Few men, lone cottages, cattle, a handful of sheep, and a bunched line of children with steaming breath cycling to school ahead of the teacher.

By Hayes' Cross, from behind the hedgerow, big Mick Connors booms "Hello, Niall." He is settling his bicycle under shelter in the field, stowing away his lunch and untying the shovel and slasher that he will use on the ditches along that stretch of the roadside today. He knows these roads, and daily sets off on his bicycle around the parish to clean out drains and slash back high encroaching bushes. As he knows every drain and every handy spot for storing a bicycle during the day, so, too, he knows the people who come and go along the roads as he works on quietly by himself. And we know him: a big man with a heavy arm waving and calling a friendly hello from inside the ditch.

"Morning, Mick."

"Cold enough today, Niall?"

"It is."

"That's right. But it made no frost, thank God."

"No, Mick," I say, cycling slowly past, as I do every morning, our daily fragment of conversation like a bright paper caught on the hedgerow.

At Cotter's Hill, where the road winds steeply upwards and a gushing rivulet crosses the road's surface to the ditch on the lower side, the children get off and walk and chat. I wobble past them and they smile and call:

"Morning, sir."

"Morning."

"Looking well on the bike today, sir."

The Honans' three geese cross the road in front of the bicycles and plap through the gap into the Duggans'. It is nine o'clock. Turf smoke is already curling from the houses in the village. There is a noise of children from the school. Here, from beyond the corners of the waking parish this morning, from farm and village house alike, have come nearly 250 students. They push and chat and chase around the school. Buses from Mullagh, Cooraclare, and Cree, the farm villages down the road, let them off before the bell and then, at five past nine, they disappear into the building and the countryside grows quiet once more.

Outside the school, in the surrounding countryside, things happen slowly, unobtrusively: a man carries a bart of hay on his shoulder, another cleans out a ditch, a woman cycles in coat and headscarf to ten o'clock mass. They are figures in the landscape, fragments of its life, as much as the slow free movement of the animals in the fields or the birds coming and going, disturbing nothing. Sometimes a tractor passes, or the cattle in Honan's field come down to the ditch overlooking the school's four new rooms. Rain falls.

This mid-November morning the country is only a few days away from a general election. But in the West Clare countryside there is no quickened, expectant feel to the morning nor the splash of strong colored posters and bill-boards as in the towns and cities. Rather, there is an over-whelming sense of things remaining the same. A sort of dull ache. The fields beyond their hedgerows in the soft damp fist of winter, the sucking sounds of cattle hooves in the muck by the hay feeder, the whole imperturbable fabric of the place bespeaks changelessness. Here you may easily imagine nothing has changed in years; that nothing can change. The countryside is still composed of small farms and cottages, poor fields and wraparound misty rain. It takes only the slightest leap of imagination for a hundred years to drop away, to hear the clap of horse and cart, to see the heads of a man and a woman passing above the hedgerows as they are drawn at a trot on their way to Kilmihil village, passing the same grazing cattle, the same lulled hush on the landscape, the same rain falling.

This morning at St. Michael's, Kilmihil's secondary school, I ask my class of sixteen- and seventeen-year-old boys and girls what they think of the election. Who would *they* vote for? The newspapers and television commentators are unanimous in declaring it one of the most critical elections the country has ever faced, an election that will shape the Ireland of the year 2000 and direct us through the oncoming years of greater European unity. The answers from the class, slow in coming, are: "What does it matter, sir?" "Aren't they all the one thing anyway?" "I'll take whichever one of 'em's going to give me a job." "I wouldn't vote for any of 'em. None of 'em is going to do anything for Kilmihil."

Not surprisingly perhaps, the state of the nation is not mentioned directly by the students but it is ever-present in their comments. For here in West Clare as in all the other small farming communities up and down the west coast of the country there is a lack of expectancy that is now almost a part of growing up for these students, the unspoken yet certain knowledge that of this classroom of thirty there are jobs in Clare for less than ten, jobs in Ireland for only a handful more. Their brothers and sisters are already spread out in the world, returning as visitors at Christmas or in summertime. I can feel keenly in this classroom how politics have failed them.

These are sons and daughters of farmers, teachers, tradesmen, and shopkeepers, and if there is no job at home, no trade to move into, no farm to take over, no place in college, they must emigrate. It is as simple as that. And so, for many of them there has developed, alongside the feeling of pride in their own place, a stronger longing to escape. When I ask them, foolishly, if they would stay at home if there *were* jobs for them, they look at me with a blank emptiness born of too much disappointment and too much reality. Am I mad? What is the point in thinking about that? They have long since stopped dreaming that dream.

I am trying to sound optimistic and hopeful for them when Larry Blake knocks and enters the classroom. Larry is the school principal, and, along with his wife, Lucy, one of our best friends in the village. He is a short solid figure of a man with thick silver hair and blue eyes. His expression slips naturally into a smile and he's never far from an easy laugh. At fifty-nine he takes the world as he finds it. He has been principal at the school for over twenty years and in that time more than doubled the enrollment and built several extensions to the original building, including a modern gym, football field, and running track, making it one of the finest schools in the country. Everybody knows Larry Blake. He's a man, they say, who gets things done. But he's also a man who enjoys people, and this morning there's a smile in his eyes as he interrupts my class.

"Lady here for you, Niall."

"Who is it, Larry?"

"Oh, a visitor," he grins. "She's above in my office."

"Should I ask her to wait until after my class?"

Larry shakes his head at my even posing the question. "There's no problem, Niall. No problem," he says, one of his favorite expressions. And, after a pause, he adds "She's from California."

I leave the class to him for a minute and go down the corridor. A reader from America awaits me, someone who has been sharing our life through three books now and has come to see us, to see the village, the townland, and the house: to touch the reality of what seemed, from far away, the *romance* of our life in Clare. Mary from California is in Larry's office. She is a slim middle-aged woman in a lavender tracksuit with a tanned face and ash blond hair, a woman who has stepped right out of American suburbia and landed in rural Ireland. I am aware as I am talking to her how "foreign" she must seem to the pupils passing by.

"I'm so sorry, Mr. Williams, for disturbing you. That man didn't tell me you were busy."

"No, it's all right."

"This is amazing, you know? Being here like this. It really is. Because I've been planning this trip for a year. When I read your first book I loved it, really, and I said to my sister, That's where I want to go, you know? In that lovely place, that's where I want to be."

"Kilmihil?"

"Yes."

She beams with pleasure as we stand there in the cramped office. She has, thoughtfully, brought us a bag of California wildflower seeds for the garden.

Now, almost ten years later, the words we once wrote are still coming back to us through just such visitors, and through them we keep meeting our younger selves. It may be the nature of Ireland itself, for it is the kind of country that keeps coming back to you even when you have left it behind. Its peace and wet greenery attach themselves like vines to the memory of the traveller; an Ireland of the imagination takes over. I know this so well for I had felt it myself years earlier on rainy streets in Manhattan, and indeed, with Chris, had abandoned one life for another partly from just such a feeling.

"But, Mary," I wanted to say, "it is still a struggle. Life here in the West is difficult. Money is tight, it's hard to get things done, my pupils see no future for themselves at home, and at eighteen our two children will be leaving, too, in all likelihood. What will happen then? And will it have been worth it? Will the quality of these years in which we try to make a life of peace and safety, of beauty, of gardening and painting and writing and teaching and the drama group and the animals and the neighbors and all the other pieces of this 'country living' add up to what we had longed for and imagined it to be all those years ago?"

But I just thank Mary for the gift of the wildflower seeds and say good-bye.

What I have not said to Mary is that our own future in Clare is only slightly more secure than that of the students at St. Michael's. When we first came to Kilmihil we had hoped that farming and writing together could support us. And for our first three years our little herd of four cows—purchased for £2000—brought in a modest income through the sale each October of their weanling calves. For each of the cows in calf we bought a second calf, and when the cows had reared them through the summer, we had sometimes eight calves for sale. Each of them was worth around £300. It was not a lot of money for a year's work. But we had always intended it to be a supplement, not a sole income. Then, in the spring of 1990, we bought three heifer calves at £180 each with a young black bull for £250. Through that wet summer they were suckled by our cows—Brigit, Susie, Phoebe, and Gerty—along with the Kiltumper calves. But at the end of October, when we went to sell them at Ennis Mart, they made slightly less than what we had paid for them. It was a hard lesson, but a necessary one. The cows were not a hobby, they took time and work, they needed minding and care, fencing in, moving. And the bought-in calves needed to be watched in the summer to be sure the adoptive mothers let them feed. It was work we loved doing—but not something we could afford any longer.

Nor is ours a lone case. The lot of the small farmer in the west of Ireland is an increasingly difficult one. The day of the farm with three or four cows and a small kitchen garden is gone. The whole viability of farming as an enterprise in places like West Clare is now in question. The land is poor, and the European Community market to which Ireland now belongs, highly competitive.

In mainland Europe cattle are kept in pasture for a minimum time and fed in vast concrete farmyards for most of the year. "The 'concrete cow' gives a lot of milk," a farmer observed to me. Due to an oversupply of milk within the EC, it has been impossible for some years now for a new farmer to go into dairying, or for a dairy farmer to expand. Milk quotas are fixed and offers are made by the Department of Agriculture to buy the quotas back from farmers so as to lower production. And so the small farmer stays small, existing largely on a system of government grants and headage payments. Farming then, for many people, must be looked at as a way of life, but not a way of making a living. In recognition of this hard fact, Chris and I sold the cows one spring morning in 1991 and said good-bye to the days when we walked up the hill fields to count the calves or bring them a bale of hay. We have a mare, Nancy, and a donkey, Nellie, and Max, the cat, and a clutch of hens around the yard. But the hills of Kiltumper are planted now with tiny oak and ash trees, bare sticks in the wintertime.

My job at St. Michael's is not secure either. I teach English and French part-time this year. But the school is under the national pupil-teacher ratio of twenty-five to one. There are just 244 pupils. For any prospect of a full-time post, that number would need to increase by at least thirty—this in an area where the population trend is one of precipitous decline.

So, like many others living in the West, we face the need to make the mosaic of our life from different pieces. More and more farmers have turned to farm tourism and home enterprise as ways of supplementing their dwindling incomes, and we have come to realize that we must write about our life in order to continue living it.

Just before we sold the cows, I began writing a play. For a while Chris and I worked on the script together. When it was announced that the National Writers Workshop that year was to be in drama, with Garry Hynes (a woman whose work I greatly admire and the new artistic director of the Abbey Theatre in Dublin) as its moderator, I submitted that script.

A month later, I was in Galway, one of eight writers selected to participate in the workshop. We met in a hotel in November, the eight of us, four men and four women from different parts of the country: two film directors, a radio scriptwriter, two women poets, an unemployed Dublin housepainter with three unproduced scripts, a priest-novelist, and me. The first night we sat around a long table in Neactain's upstairs restaurant, off Shop Street, and waited to meet with Garry Hynes. A small curly-headed woman in her late thirties with intense brown eyes, wearing a black leather jacket and jeans and chain-smoking, appeared: a stranger upon whom all our expectations and hopes were focussed.

We met for several weekends in Galway over the course of that winter. I began a first play of my own called *The Murphy Initiative*, a three-act comedy about the changing relationships between America and Ireland. I was the only one in the group working on a comedy—the other plays in progress were dramas of social injustice, full of intensity and explosive passion. After each workshop I returned to Chris and Deirdre in Kiltumper.

"Well," Chris would ask, "did you read out any of it? What did Garry think?"

"No, I didn't read it. It's not ready yet."

"But you're dying to know what she thinks of it."

"Yes."

"And it's a workshop. It doesn't have to be ready."

"It's the only comedy," I said. "I'm not sure it's any good."

"At least ask *her* to read it," Chris urged me.

On the last day of the workshop, in March 1991, four actors came to the upstairs rehearsal room of the tiny Druid

Theatre in Galway and read aloud the first act of *The Murphy Initiative*. It went extraordinarily well, the lines bubbling along and the laughter coming easily.

TB: Listen. Billy the Kid?

SHAMIE: What?

TB: Billy the Kid, Irish. Jesse James?

SHAMIE: Yeah?

TB: Father from Kerry. Irish. Buffalo Bill? Butch Cassidy? Audie Murphy, Henry Ford, JFK? Irish. Not a decent outlaw anywhere that wasn't some part Irish. And Eamon De Valera?

SHAMIE: An outlaw?

TB: An American. Born in New York, cowboy. Them and Us, like that (interlinks his fingers). Think about that when you're riding outa town.

When it was over I could hear the buzz of my first audience. Garry sat curled into a deep armchair with a cigarette and asked for opinions. Her own came last, "Well, Niall, the hardest thing now will be to come up with a second act as good."

I phoned Chris from Galway that afternoon before I drove home, intoxicated by the dream of one day having my play staged in a theatre.

Chris sat before the open hearth in the cottage one evening in April to read the first draft of the whole play. In a small village in the West, desperation has brought a county councilman and a local businessman to create "an initiative" whereby American visitors named Murphy are duped into believing that an old abandoned cowhouse is, in fact, their ancestral home. It is a play about the "roots" industry in Ireland, the selling of grandfathers and of home hearths; a play about the entangled relationships between Ireland and America, how we mutually trade to fulfill our different needs. Ireland provides the history, the sense of belonging, the roots, and America, the dollars and the mirror in which we look at ourselves. Above all, though, I think of it as a play about people driven to extremes. For when there is nothing else to sell to keep a community alive, it must sell its past.

Chris said, when she had finished reading it, "Send it to Garry tomorrow."

We went down to the village, to post the manuscript together, borne upon a great tide of hope and anxiety. For the play, although not directly about our lives, did touch upon them. And we hoped it would be the means by which we could manage to continue living in Kiltumper.

Gregory, the postmaster, was on the phone when we rushed into the post office. A man of fifty with a dry wit, he loves horses. He had fallen from a horse and broken his pelvis a few months earlier. The moment he fell, it was widely reported, he had stood up, in agony, ready to mount the horse again. He had just gotten off his crutches and moved very slowly and deliberately.

I handed him the envelope as he got off the phone and he weighed it.

"That'll cost a bit then," he said.

"How much, Gregory?"

"Off to the Abbey Theatre, are we?"

"That's right."

"I suppose it won't be long till we're after it?"

"Please God," I said, and Chris added, "Please Garry."

"Well, how does £3.24 grab you?" And so, it was mailed off to Dublin.

After that, silence. No word. Every few days I drove to the university in Galway sixty miles away to complete my courses for a teaching diploma so that I might be eligible for full-time work at the high school—should any become available. I arrived home each evening to find Chris and Deirdre still waiting for news from Dublin.

I had more or less concluded that nothing was going to happen when I came in the back door one evening three weeks later and saw, on a long banner hung from the kitchen ceiling, words that Chris and Deirdre had crayoned: CON-GRATULATIONS. SHE LOVES IT!!! In May 1991 the Abbey Theatre in Dublin purchased *The Murphy Initiative*.

First and new plays usually premiered downstairs in the Peacock Theatre, a smaller theatre. One evening in June, Garry telephoned to tell me that she wanted my play to open in August on the main stage. Chris and I could hardly believe it. We danced around the kitchen floor that bright May evening, and the struggle of life in Kiltumper faded away. A first play on the main stage of the Abbey Theatre! What incredible luck!

In the two months before rehearsals began, our life took another unexpected leap forward. We had been on a waiting list with the adoption agency for three years and had all but given up the hope of being able to give Deirdre a brother or sister. Only a week earlier Chris and I had sat in a café in

Ennis and wondered how long we would keep ourselves on the waiting list. We supposed that, with the decreasing number of children placed for adoption in Ireland, the first preference was given to childless couples, and we had decided to wait until the end of the summer. If it wasn't meant to be . . .

Then on the last day of May the phone rang. Chris answered it. It was the social worker with Clarecare in Ennis, the umbrella organization that now included the adoption agency.

"Are you sitting down, Christine?"

"Should I?"

"Well, we'd like you and Niall to come in and meet a birth mother."

Later that week we met a young woman in the Clarecare center. Seated in a small room with the blinds pulled against the dazzling afternoon sunlight was a fair-haired woman of twenty-five with composed blue eyes. Only the action of her hands searching in her bag for a cigarette betrayed her ordeal. On April 1 she had given birth to a boy she called Daire— "Meaning oak," she said. "I wanted something strong." She asked us questions about ourselves. She was studying journalism and wanted to know the child would be adopted by a couple who valued books and education.

When we were introduced we had not used our surnames. We met concealed behind a thin veil of anonymity. But, knowing that my play was about to be staged and that my picture would be published in the theatre sections of Irish newspapers, I asked her if she felt enough at peace with her decision that, though she might learn where the child lived, she could leave him to his new life.

"Yes," she said, and after a pause added, "once I make up my mind, I'll be happy with my decision."

In June, just two weeks before I left for rehearsals in Dublin, Chris and I drove to Ennis with Deirdre, telling her of the same journey we had taken four years earlier to the adoption agency for her. She became a big sister in a moment, moving as children do from one phase to the next before it seems possible. In the same small room with the blinds closed, the three of us sat and waited in our best clothes, and just before lunchtime we were handed a baby boy, whom we named Joseph Daire.

As an infant he sat propped up, almost entirely hairless, a Buddha child raising his eyebrows, his main expression one of wonder in reaction to the world in which he had arrived. Light attracted him; he searched out the light bulbs in the room with his eyes and sometimes pointed at lights we couldn't see. He was almost holy in his serenity in those first months.

Big, placid, and blue-eyed, he arrived in the house even as one of its walls was falling down. We needed more room; the existing "back kitchen," as we called it, was an unheated addition with a corrugated roof, built onto the house like a lean-to thirty years earlier. Almost from the time we first moved into the cottage Chris had been planning *her* kitchen, rendering a series of sketches and floor plans during the long winter evenings, which were put aside year after year, waiting for the time when we could afford it. Now, with the news of the play and the arrival of the baby, we borrowed money and went ahead.

The three-foot-thick gable wall on the western end of the cottage was broken through—to a clatter of loose stones, three men's shoulders under a steel girder, and some of the upstairs coming downstairs, as Chris picked up Joseph and ran outside into the garden. Little by little the great gaping hole in the side of the cottage became the passageway into the new kitchen. The decor was to be simple: Everything was to be as natural as possible, and constructed largely of old materials. The flooring was to be wooden and old wood at that—one afternoon Chris and I had walked around a yard near the Dublin docks and picked out some dusty pitch pine boards, "Complete with the old nail holes, d'y'see there?" They had been brought down to Kilmihil by a neighbor in the back of an empty ice-cream trailer.

The counters and cabinets were no less individual. Through Gerry, a good friend married to Michael, our family doctor, we had heard of a carpenter and cabinetmaker named Fran, who lived in Miltown Malbay, ten miles to the west. He made new dressers from old ones, we had been told, working in the small garage adjoining his house. From the moment we visited him—a very tall easygoing man in his thirties, stooping and running his fingers lightly over the grain and finish of different pieces as he spoke—we loved Fran's work. He was a shy man who spoke hesitantly with a Dublin accent and hated to mention prices.

"Yeah, came down originally for the music. Liked the pace, the kids loved it. Like holidays at first, it was. We're here eight or nine years now, 'bout the same as yourselves?" He paused. "But it never gets any easier, does it?" He shrugged off the difficulties. "Well, I can make you lovely countertops now, Chris, from the seats of some old pews I got in Kilrush. I haven't got too much of it, but there might be enough."

With its nail-holed floor, pew counters, the dresser that

was bits old and new, eight-foot-wide sliding doors, and a skylight in the arched pine ceiling, the new kitchen was a place of light and wood and welcome. Then Chris found an ad in the newspaper for reconditioned Aga stoves, and a man called Finian arrived in his overalls, looking part-boiler himself. He carried in, piece by cast-iron piece, the twin ovens and heavy heating and simmering plates, and the black, comforting and constant heart of the room was in place.

A new baby, a new room, and a play at the Abbey, Ireland's national theater. In July as I travelled up to Dublin for rehearsals I could not have been a happier man. I was, of course, full of tension, an outsider in this new world of rehearsal rooms and production planning. Moreover, I had a very keen sense of myself as *coming up from the country*. It was absurd. I was born a Dubliner and had only been living in Clare for six years. And yet, arriving at the Abbey Theatre I felt that I was crossing some imaginary threshold and landing in the capital city as someone else, the country bumpkin. "He lives down in Clare," was the first thing Lucy, the publicist, said, introducing me around. And "*He lives down in Clare*" became the handle affixed to me, as Kiltumper took on a kind of bucolic mythos, a wash of pastoral greens concealing our actual lives, imagined now as jolly walks up the fields and playing about in the garden.

This misperception was not shared by Garry Hynes. For Garry had experienced a similar reaction. She came to Dublin from the West as the most exciting theater director in the country, having co-founded the Druid Theatre in Galway, been its first artistic director, and been largely responsible for its rise to prominence. She came "up" to Dublin from the west of Ireland, and it seems that implicit in her hiring was some sense that the quality of her productions at Druid had benefitted from what Dublin imagined to be the natural poetry of life in the West. Galway remains the most romantic city in the country. It is on the Atlantic; has narrow winding streets; cobbled alleyways; wonderful dark, dim, smoky pubs; Kenny's extraordinary bookshop; the oyster festival; the arts festival; and more besides. It is alive and thriving, and in bringing Garry Hynes to Dublin to the National Theatre, there was some attempt to bring that Galway mystique to the capital, to enliven the Abbey.

When I came up in July, the Abbey was already astir with controversy. Garry's first production, of Sean O'Casey's classic *The Plough and the Stars*, had not been a traditional one. The performance was set upon a severely raked stage, characters had shaven or closely cropped heads, and a huge Union Jack banner was hung across the proscenium. The newspapers were buzzing; opinions were sharply divided. Either it was a brilliant new interpretation of the text or it was a complete insult to the memory of one of the Abbey's principal writers and his greatest play. Garry took the controversy in her stride, and the production, through its extraordinary notoriety, sold tickets at a rapid clip. My play was to follow on the same stage soon after.

Throughout the rehearsals I never lost the feeling of being the writer "up from Clare." The actors and the director, Paul Mercier, kept asking me about the world of the play— the places, the people. But when I answered, describing a village in my imagination, I could see it become to them this *wonderful place down there in Clare.* It was funny and full of odd characters and great sayings and mad situations; it was wonderful—but it was not real. The reality of the place and my conception of the play vanished somewhere in the middle of July. It is something that has puzzled me every day since: How exactly did it happen? How did I let it get away from me? For what followed was like a sudden downhill crash in a car from which I couldn't escape. Vivid moments like shards of glass lodge in my memory: The first night of previews, being drawn aside in the bar and told "You know, you've written a terrific play, but this production doesn't represent it." The busload of people who came from Kilmihil, travelling across the country and back in the same night to lend their support, bringing lumps to my throat with gratitude, reminding me whom I was writing for. The opening night when a great coolness like the breeze from a low-powered fan wafted through the auditorium, as Irish celebrities looked sideways across at each other to gauge each other's reactions. Intermission in the tiny VIP lounge crowded with people including the board of the theater, when only Garry spoke to Chris and me. We stood there, like people attending our own executions. The *Irish Times* review the following morning was headlined: TOTAL AND EMBARRASSING WASTE OF A BAD IDEA.

Not all the reviews were negative. The play completed its scheduled run of four weeks and audiences came and enjoyed it. But it had lost its point and become simply a broad comedy. Later, back in Clare, I could blame no one but myself. Certainly the play had many faults. It was my first and I thought it would be my last.

Garry stood by me as best she could, urging me to begin

anew. The local people in Kilmihil who had seen the play were quick to tell me how they had enjoyed it. But I came back to Clare, and Chris and the children in the new kitchen, heavy with a sense of failure. Mentions of the play, usually in connection with words like "debacle" or "disaster," continued to float through theater articles for the rest of the year, and the *Irish Times* gave the production its award for Worst Moment in Theater, 1991.

Nonetheless, I spent the next year writing a new play called *A Little Like Paradise*. It's about the same western village, struggling to survive, and a man, Lazarus Maguire, who dies in the local pub and then wakes up again. And when it was finished, I sent it to Garry in Dublin. And now, once more, we are waiting to hear.

Tonight, as the gift of Mary's California wildflower seeds lies in a cellophane bag on the dresser, the cottage seems loosely moored by dreamlike threads running to America and Dublin. The rain and wind are thrashing the tall bare sycamore trees that stand along the western wall of the hay barn. Down the chimney and across the eight-foot hearth of the great fireplace in the center of the cottage spit black melting hailstones. They spatter across the vinyl on the floor or hiss into the turf; we don't pay them much notice anymore. The old pine shutters are closed against the night, but if you could stand in the dark kitchen and peer out at the countryside, the sweep of the valley you know is there would seem to be nothing but wind and rain. The house feels the weather on all sides of it. The lights flicker, as they always do in advance of a blackout, and I go down to the children's room at the end of the house. They are sleeping on through the storm. I leave the lights on and hope that Deirdre or Joseph won't wake to a blackout. It seems suddenly a terrible thing to me—a child, afraid, waking in the dark in the middle of a storm in the country. Deirdre, when younger, always wanted me to stand at the doorway to the bedroom as she fell asleep, and I had often done so, waiting, watching until she slept, before slipping away, feeling like a thief moving back through the house. What was I protecting her from in sleep? Dreams would slip past me in the doorway. There were no monsters. And yet, it felt right to stand there, listening to the children breathing, as I thought of Mary's wildflower seeds, of the play sent to Dublin, the country waiting to vote, and our endeavors to continue to make our life in Kiltumper.

The lights flicker but don't go out. The rain beats on.

CHRISTINE'S JOURNAL:

For several minutes I watched the last yellow leaf of Joseph's tulip tree in a wild dance in the middle of a heavy November shower. The rain came quickly down, pounding upon us as I was writing at the big oak table in the kitchen this morning. The carved table, an antique that belonged to my grandmother, my father's Irish mother, has more or less found its place here with us in Kiltumper. It belongs here in front of the window offering us not only a spot from which to view the slope of the garden but also another connection to this place.

Like a swallow, with notched wings and lobed sides, the leaf soared and dove, secured to its branch, graceful and strong. I watched it for minutes, feeling the storm surround me, the racing cold rain and the wind, my little shelter inside the house just barely protecting me. I am one of those people who hate the wintry wind, but at least in the daylight I am more able to bear it, and as I sat marveling at the power of this leaf against the wind that I feared, it suddenly let go and darted madly to the ground. It was like watching a falling star.

The tulip tree, *liriodondron tulipfera*, stands leafless now, no longer needing to nourish its leaves but able to devote its full energy to surviving winter. Late next spring its leaves will bloom again and someday, seven winters from now, when Joseph is about eight, little green and cream tuliplike flowers will form.

Unlike the tree, I have yet to learn how to put aside my summer dress with such grace and strength and acceptance. I seem to forge into winter with mad summer energy still clinging to me. I know it is I who needs to learn to let go.

Perhaps it will take seven more winters.

✦ Two ✦

West Clare is a peninsula of land bordered by the estuary of the River Shannon to the south and the rugged Atlantic coastline to the north and west. Its principal town is Kilrush, a farming and market center built on the banks of the Shannon. As you leave Ennis and head west along the Kilrush road, the countryside opens out into green pastures, but then, ten miles from Ennis, the fields lose their color and the land shows its poverty, becoming low-lying and rushy with brown boglands interspersed between the fields. The road itself rises and falls, and on the almost thirty miles to Kilrush I always think of the man who told me there is more gravel in this road than any in the country, for it's built, he said, over pure bog and keeps sinking. It's easy to believe as the car moves like a boat along its ripples. As the land gets poorer—reds and browns in the winter light—so the farms seem to shrink.

This is the land of small holdings: There are many farms of less than thirty acres of boggy ground. The population is aging, and families of eight, nine, and ten children are no more. In Clare as a whole the population decline is in line with the national average of 0.5 percent, but in West Clare the figure is 7.4 percent. The greatest proportion of the population loss comes from the eighteen- to forty-four-year-old age group. When you drive along the small back roads there are many empty cottages. Farmers in their seventies sell off their fields, for their children, gone to Dublin or London or The Bronx, are not going to return to farm them. The only viable farms in West Clare now are the bigger ones.

In Kilmihil, our village, three miles in from the Ennis-to-Kilrush road, there are three hundred families. The majority still make some of their living from farming, but in many cases the wife works outside the home in Ennis or Kilrush, or the farmer only farms in the very early morning and when he returns in the evening from the factories at Shannon or the electricity-generating station at Moneypoint near Kilrush. Still, Kilmihil remains largely a farming community. More than three-quarters of the families live on or work the home farm. The average farm size is fifty-five acres, though in each of the townlands around the parish there are a handful of farmers who have bought and taken over neighboring lands and now run viable farms of almost two hundred acres.

West Clare, like other rural farming areas in the west, has

traditionally been the territory of Fianna Fail—the Republican Party, the largest party in the country and the one that has most frequently held power in the past. A few years ago the party slipped from a position of overall majority and was forced to go into coalition with the smaller party of the Progressive Democrats.

Who we in Clare vote for is not a burning issue for the rest of the country, especially for Dubliners. To them it seems to go without saying: We are all farmers down here, aren't we? Of course we'll all be voting for Fianna Fail.

This time I am not so sure. All that seems certain is the awareness in the West of the need for something better. For while urban centers have grown rapidly the rural communities have declined—in population and services. In the ten years since Chris and I moved to Clare we have seen very little development—our roads have gotten worse, our hospital in Ennis has been gradually downgraded and the maternity ward closed down so that now it is impossible to have a child born in the county of Clare. Instead, cars with pregnant mothers speed by on the busy road to Limerick or Galway.

On the radio and in the newspapers one word stands out from the other slogans of the election: *change*. Bill Clinton had just won his election riding on the power of the same word. Change: The thing nobody can speak against, even those in power. It is being invoked almost like a spell by the Labor Party, offered as the antidote to whatever political malaise the country has been suffering, its potency directly proportionate to the illness. Prior to the election Labor had only seventeen seats in a house of 162. In November 1992 thirty-two Labor candidates are running. In the days before the election, Labor's leader, Dick Spring, a tall well-groomed man moving through the streets in a long overcoat, is, according to the polls, the most popular leader in the country. (He, too, is married to an American.)

Two weeks before the election, Fianna Fail, feeling threatened, ran a series of advertisements warning that a vote for Labor was a vote for increased spending, property taxes, wealth taxes, and, in short, the ruination of the country. But a vote for Fianna Fail meant everything good.

In the days before voting the promises have come thick and strong: free university for all, the abolishment of fees, the building of the long-delayed hospital in Tallaght (a suburb of Dublin that has swelled to the size of a small city).

And still, that word keeps cropping up. Vote for: *change*.

By evening time on election day I had not yet voted. I had come home from school to the cottage, dispirited. There was still no news from Garry Hynes at the Abbey. And Joseph had fallen on the rough, potholed, and rocky road that runs past our house, opening a deep wound in his forehead. For over a month Chris had been asking me to write again to our local councillors to complain about it. It is one of the worst roads anywhere. The top surface has long since been washed away and the original stones of the foundations stick up jagged or bumpy. I had not gotten around to the letter, half-affected by the sense I encountered too often that nothing could be done, and half by the hope that I would come home one day to find the road there, waiting, resurfaced, proving that local government worked, that there was money even for small rural communities whose roads were washing away. But Joseph, with a deep gash in his forehead, was all that was waiting.

It is still raining in the same slow drizzling way when I drive to Deirdre's school to vote. Mine are the only head-lights that pierce the blanket of dark, illuminating the wet road before me as I drive around the bad bend to where the lights in the master's room blaze out over the small school-yard. I stop the car by the ditch on the narrow road and go in.

"Evening, Niall," Helena Ryan, our smiling young butcher from down in the village, greets me. Helena is in her twenties and has only recently taken over from her father, whose meat business was located in the front of the family bar. Marty's, as it had been known for so long, was famous for quality meat. When we first arrived in Kilmihil, we were told Marty knew how to hang meat, and it was true. There was something special in what he sold at the shop—although sometimes the vision of our butcher in his stained white coat slipping behind the counter of the bar and pulling a pint was a little too *surreal* for us. When he retired and Helena took over there was some doubt that the customers would take to a lady butcher. As it turned out, the business has improved. Helena has raised the standard of hygiene and display in the shop. Now, after a couple of years, she is as much a figure of village life as her father.

Today she has a trainee looking after the shop while she works at the polling station. "It's a great break," she says, looking down the list of voters in the Clonigulane district to find my name. "And you know, it's different when you're sitting up here in a classroom. It's very different from being down in the village."

Along the road that comes from the village, curving toward the hills of Glenmore and the bogs of Kilmaley, live 111 constituents. Since early that morning they have been coming in cars, tractors, and on foot, into the same master's room where many of them had received their first education. Three people, overseeing the polling, are sitting at the small desks facing the blackboard. They look strangely comical to me: adults, oversized in the children's room, their legs sticking out into the aisle and hands resting on the old carved wood of desks that have been there for almost half a century.

There are two ballot sheets. One, for the election to the Irish legislature, the Dail; a second one for the abortion referendum, which itself has three parts: one, the right to have an abortion in Ireland; two, access to information on abortion, which had hitherto been illegal; and, three, the right to travel abroad for an abortion, a right that had recently been denied a pregnant teenage victim of rape. The very idea of such a referendum, with a likely outcome *No, Yes, Yes,* seems indicative of the country's struggle with change.

In front of the blackboards are two three-sided ballot boxes made of chipboard. Doorless, curtainless, they face the class like upright open caskets. Step inside one and you might be standing in your own last place. Inside, a small pencil hangs on a string. Nothing else. A simple plain place. Within the box, because of its very plainness perhaps, I can feel the power in the pencil.

The sheet for the election of Dail members carries thirteen names to be numbered in order of preference. There are four seats to be won in Clare. For these there are four Fianna Fail candidates, three Fine Gael candidates, two Progressive Democrats, one Labor, and three Independents, who are running without party endorsement. As I grasp the pencil I hear the wind pick up outside. Rain begins beating more heavily on the long, dark windows of the classroom. Despite all the newspaper and television coverage I still have not quite decided whom to vote for; the election seems in equipoise. If you believe change is possible, it seems, you vote Labor; if you believe, more cynically, as in my classroom down in the school, that one crowd is as bad as the next, then you vote to leave things as they are. Or so I see it, standing there in the master's room in the November night with the wind blowing rain across the West Clare landscape.

In a mood of affirmation and hope—a mood that I hope is pulsing tonight throughout the length and breadth of the country—I take the pencil and look down at the name of the Labor candidate listed on the sheet. He is the practicing psychiatrist at Our Lady's Hospital in Ennis, a South African-born Indian who married a woman from the neighboring parish of Cooraclare over twenty years ago. There have been jokes and stories circulating about Dr. Moosajee Bhamjee all week, put about mostly by his opponents. How, if elected, he will forgo a state car—would prefer an elephant instead; how he's secretly hoping not to be elected, and if anyone votes for him they'll need their head examined—and he'll do it free of charge; how the Labor Party only put him up for the election at the last minute because Dick Spring thought it would promote a positive image for the party; and how, truly, they all thought the man was bananas. I have heard all these stories but also of Dr. Bhamjee the family man, the man with children in Ennis, who cares about what's happening in the Clare community, who wears a heavy coat to protect him from the Irish winter as he stands on the sidelines of Sunday soccer matches in the parks in Ennis, who spoke compassionately to a meeting Chris attended of voluntary Samaritans. He is a man who came as the quintessential outsider to County Clare, and has made it his home.

I take the pencil and write number one beside his name.

Two days after the election, votes were still being counted this morning in the West County Hotel in Ennis. There is still no result, and the country is held rapt in the telly glow of predictions, first counts, second counts, and transfers. The proportional representation system itself seems at once archaic and peculiarly our own political madness, defying even the computers. The tallymen, party members whose expert eyes flicker over the ballot sheets as they are unfolded on the tables, are the closest thing to real information. In the halls and hotels up and down the country where the counting buzzes on, it is from them that the rumors of those elected or defeated first emanate—"We're hearing of an upturn in the west"; "Not looking good for Fianna Fail in North Dublin." Over and over the same ballot papers are counted and recounted; each time the last candidate is eliminated second preference votes are transferred to the remaining candidates. And so on it has gone for two days. And more counting, and more, as bleary-eyed politicians and their handlers press through hotel doors into the early-morning halls to stand around and sit and drink more coffee and wait.

And the more we wait the more it seems that something is really happening here. There is that word again: change. After the second count, the Dublin news reports Dr. Bhamjee of Clare is in a relatively strong position. Two of the four sitting government members are in a serious contest to hold their seats. But it will be lunchtime before a clearer picture emerges.

I went to school this morning with a feeling of anticipation. Chris was even more excited, for she sees a strong showing by Dr. Bhamjee as a sign not solely of protest against the previous ministers but as an indication of something hopeful and tolerant. That a county like Clare with a large rural community can break from the traditions of the past and change, to have not only a "foreigner"—albeit one who has lived in Clare for twenty-odd years—but a Labor candidate as its representative, seems remarkable.

There was no one without an opinion on the good doctor in the village today. The jokes of a week earlier took on a different shade as the "No Hope" candidate, the token protest man, the man who I was told would get no more than a thousand votes, now looked as if he might become the first South African, the first "colored" man to be elected to our national legislature. There was amazement in the air. And humor too.

During the afternoon, in the heat and smoke of the West County Hotel, Dr. Bhamjee was declared elected to Dail Eireann! Immediately Clare shot into national headlines: WHAT HAS HAPPENED IN CLARE? And although in the country itself the same picture emerged as Labor candidate after candidate made gains, with Labor winning an unprecedented number of seats, no victory seemed more celebrated than Dr. Bhamjee's. Racist jokes were circulating within hours of his election, yet their malice was dispelled by the man himself, as he shrugged and laughed and said to an interviewer for RTE, Irish radio, after his election: "Now there'll be an Indian among the cowboys. Oh yes," he added, with a broad grin, "it's a black day for Ireland."

"We're all delighted down here over Dr. Bhamjee," I said tonight on the phone to a friend in Dublin.

"Sure that fella's a complete headcase."

A complete headcase; it may be the perfect synonym for the Ennis psychiatrist. But it is also a measure of the difference between up there and down here, between the politics of the urban center of the country and the tangible longing for attention of a place where the old certainties are no longer working, and where there is a feeling sometimes of being unrepresented in Dublin, cut adrift in a forgotten place.

I want to claim my Irish citizenship but I have not done so yet and so I am not entitled to vote in national elections. Still, I am finding this election very exciting and know that if I had a vote it would be a vote cast on behalf of my children's future— one that now seems all too likely to lead to emigration for them. But for the moment I am cherishing their childhoods.

Like his sister, Deirdre May, Joseph is really active and inquisitive and very alert yet there is a deep tranquility about him. Now, at the age of one and a half, Joseph is speaking in full sentences. His grasp of language is startling. He just loves to use words and seems to be intrigued by the nuance and subtlety of them. (A true Irishman, I think.) He says:

"I don't like cold tea, Mammy."

"I like warm, Mammy, not hot."

"Ohh, my tea is hotty! Mammy, hot tea."

He tries to use as many words in a sentence as he can and is not content with Pidgin English or baby talk. He even knows his pronouns and puts them to use, too. For Joseph, it's not just "me" and "mine," but "yours" and "theirs"—his teddies, JoJo Bear and Deeda Bear—and other people's. That's Joseph, not valuing his world above yours or mine. Everything is equal. He recognizes the differences and yet, to him, each is as important as the other. He has a quality about him that although natural to a baby feels and looks deeper. Like Deirdre May, Joseph has given us so much joy. It was worth the three years the three of us waited for him to come into our lives.

Deirdre is exceptionally good with Joseph and the two of them share a bond that is uniquely theirs. Deirdre and I made up a little nursery rhyme when Joseph came to us and Deirdre often says it to him:

> Cuddly Wuddly was a bear
> Cuddly Wuddly had no hair
> Cuddly Wuddly had eyes of blue
> Cuddly Wuddly, I lubaloo.

Joseph laughs. Deirdre giggles and asks him, "Are you my maribou?" Joseph says no. Deirdre asks, "Are you my caribou?" Joseph answers, "Nooooo." "Are you my kangaroo?" "Nooooo," says Joseph with a huge smile. "Then what are you?" Deirdre asks, cuddling beside Joseph, and Joseph answers with delight, "I'm your lubaloo!"

For the meantime, Niall and I are the keepers of that bond between Deirdre and Joseph, and we will guard it and nourish it daily until they grow up and treasure it themselves.

Our Christmas this year was spent in Connecticut with my brother Joe. It was little Joseph's second Christmas but his first in America. Deirdre has been back and forth across the Atlantic three times already. Now that their visas are straightened out, my two Irish children and Irish husband can travel with me whenever I feel like going "home." Yet, the idea of the United States as my home has gradually changed over the years, and *going home* isn't the same as it used to be. I feel as if I have two homes sometimes, but with Niall and the children not sharing that feeling with me, I often find myself caught between the two.

It's not an easy adjustment even after more than half a dozen years living in Ireland. I am finally beginning to settle here through the lives of Deirdre and Joseph. I see how happy they are even without all the things I miss—the distractions of American life where everything you want seems to be around the corner.

Much as I sometimes wanted it to be so, we all knew that Christmas in Connecticut for us wouldn't come every year. Next year our Christmas will be spent in Kiltumper. We will be celebrating it at home.

✦ THREE ✦

One afternoon I took a walk up through the fields behind us, moving across the Big Meadow, through the little rushy triangle of Johnny's Meadow, and up into Lower Tumper. What had been the grazing field for our first four cows and their calves had now been planted with oak and ash trees. Tree plantations—mainly of fir and pine that can be harvested for lumber within twenty-five years—were spreading quickly through the West as small farms became less viable. But for Joe, Chris's father in America, who had paid for the work, the attraction of planting oak and ash on the hillside both for their simple beauty and as a gesture against time itself was too great to resist. There had been trees on these hillsides over a thousand years ago, but it would be another forty or fifty years before this latest wood was fully grown.

A tractor track led the way across the slope of the hill now patterned by raised lines of ridges, punctuated by sticklike trees standing at angles against the wind. I saw two hares standing still between the ridges. Once I had walked these fields twice a day. Now my walks to the windy hilltop were rare, and hares are easily alarmed. Their amazement held them in place for seconds; they stopped and I stopped. Our house was only a few hundred yards down the hill; Nancy and Nellie, the mare and the donkey, were in the Big Meadow, where we went daily to feed them. And yet, the field I stood in was the creatures' now.

The hares stood and I stood. Their eyes darted but they did not run. The wind blew from the west where fields vanished and reappeared behind veils of rain mist. I tried to "become" a tree but however still I stood it was not enough. In a moment they were both gone, up the stone wall together in one smooth flowing movement and lost from sight. Still I didn't move.

For a number of years I had been part of the life of this field, coming and going from the cows. Our calves had been born up here, and we had almost lost one until together with the Downes children from down the road, we'd walked back and forth across every inch of it and finally found the tiny animal, curled asleep in a clump of rushes, and brought it back to its bellowing mother.

From up here, the view is staggering. I looked south into Kerry across the Shannon River, seeing patterns of fields, greens muddied with winter, dotted with black flecks: cattle moving before the rain, shouldering into mucky shelter under hedgerows of blackthorn, whitethorn, and gorse. Away to the west, the big sky, the Atlantic coastline, and the sense of *edge* as the land swept into a risen point I knew was Kilkee. It was raining. Not that anyone called it rain. It was not rain for closing your coat or even wearing one; it was a rain you'd see two men talking in for an hour without either of them taking shelter. And yet, as I stood there, my face was running with it. Somewhere behind me, I thought, without looking about to check, the hares were watching.

If the field had a memory, it could recall a time before the building of Tumper the Giant's grave—the ring of stones and mound on the crest of the hill. It could remember the people who lived, before the Great Famine, in what became the stone ruins of hut dwellings, remember all the cattle and their drovers. And in that memory now, for the next several decades, would be an oak and ash forest, hares and foxes and birds and pheasants and stoats and badgers, a wild place of living things. As I stood there, as still as I could, but wavering now more than the trees, from whose single clusters of leafstems dripped the slow rain, a remarkable feeling of peace descended upon me.

Earlier in the week I had read in the *Irish Times* that the writing that mythologizes the experience of the west of Ireland all comes from Dublin-based intellectuals; rural romantic places do not in fact exist. I wonder. Later, after the children were in bed, I would try and write down exactly what happened to me, upon the hill. In my journal tonight I note our financial uncertainty, the worsening of the road outside our gate, and that Joseph wakes every night, leaving

Chris and me, after our broken sleep, like fragments of ourselves the next day. No word has come from Garry Hynes about my new play. Ordinary life in the west of Ireland, in the falling rain, is lonely and a struggle. Weighed against this, I write of a walk in Upper Tumper, two hares, and a moment of magical peace. We need whatever romance we can conjure.

Driving along the Fruar Road this morning on my way into Ennis from Kiltumper I was struck by the sense of survival. I saw it all about me—in the new bungalows and in a deserted cottage being renovated, in the Friesian cows grazing on the bare, rain-soaked hills, in a single, valiant Scots pine, in the miles of stone walls still standing against the nudging of countless cattle, but most of all in the very land itself. Here in Ireland we are all survivors.

The many old abandoned stone cottages that seem to guard the roads now are not just ghosts from another age, not only signs of decline of the rural population. They, too, are symbols of survival. Their stones, taken from the clay-heavy soil two hundred years ago, will remain after I have passed by for the last time. They will still be here—hard, strong, enduring, perhaps waiting for another person in two hundred more years' time to touch them, to wonder, to rebuild. Up in Mayo the discovery of the Ceide Fields—a landscape of parallel stone walls five thousand years old—speaks eloquently of farmers who long ago chose to make a life out here on this western edge of the island, a life of hardship and endurance that still holds a lesson for us.

The Scots pine, bent and crooked, has a delightful symmetry of its own. I no longer ask it to be perfect, to grow straight and full and look like a "normal" tree. I look at it today and see beauty in its survival against the force of harsh western Atlantic winds, in its power of bending and shaping itself to the wind's pruning, in its graceful acceptance.

Who is the landscape for? One morning the radio brought us news of the latest episode in a County Clare controversy. In the Burren—a kind of natural miracle, a wild and unique habitat of limestone pavements and crag-sprung Mediterranean wildflowers sweeping to the Atlantic coastline—the people are up in arms. For as long as tourists have been visiting Clare they have been going to the Burren. With its limestone crags and narrow "grikes" or crevices, wild orchids, red-tipped bloody cranesbill, the blue harebell, the sow thistle, and other rare flowers that spring and survive between the shelves of the rock, with only birds and goats for company, the Burren is a place peopleless and hushed. Mullaghmore is a limestone mountain in the heart of the Burren; it is not especially high, but as it sits in the middle of the stretch of gray rock, like a series of gentle hoops or coils softly curving into the pale sky, it has a kind of majesty. As you drive the winding way through the Burren you keep coming upon it; it is like the magical mountain in a fairy tale: the place at the heart of mystery. Mullaghmore, like the Poulnabrone Dolmen or the Aillwee caves, is one of the principal features in the Burren. It is immediately recognizable and, therefore, more easily *marketed* than the intangible peace that is the lasting impression of having been in the Burren.

Last year, in recognition of the fact that this unique feature of the Irish landscape was totally undeveloped in terms of "amenities"—sanitary and eating facilities, as well as information for tourists—the government, through the Office of Public Works (OPW), decided to establish a Burren Interpretative Center for visitors. They promised a building in keeping with the special landscape of the Burren. And they decided to place it at the foot of Mullaghmore Mountain. At once, the Burren Action Group was founded to oppose the center while the Mullaghmore Support Committee was formed in favor of it. For the environmentalists the proposed building was an abomination. No matter how tastefully it was designed, its site, in the heart of the region, would be enough to destroy all harmony and tranquility, the very things most Burren tourists came to experience and enjoy. In addition, the water table in the limestone was likely to be polluted by effluent from the center. The road to the mountain would have to be widened and improved to make way for the tour buses, and the increase in traffic in summertime would change the slow, mazy, circuitous rambles along the Burren roads into a caterpillar line of exhaust fumes heading toward the mountain. The Burren Action Group suggested placing the proposed center on the edge of the Burren in Corofin—or in Kilfenora, where there was a small center already—instead. The OPW countered: Modern tourists want an interpretative center *at the site* of the place being interpreted. Not every tourist would have the time or desire to pass the whole day walking around the lunar landscape listening to birdsong. Most would soon be on their way to the next stop on their tour. People want to get out of their buses and cars, visit the center, and be within walking distance of whatever it was they were there to see. So the center had to be *in* the Burren, not on the edge of it.

Interestingly, many of the people who objected to the Mullaghmore center did not live in or even near the Burren. Quite a few of them did not even live in County Clare. Many were committed environmentalists from different corners of the country uniting to save Mullaghmore from government interference with a natural, national treasure.

If we had been living in Dublin, I imagine our own point of view would have been that of the environmentalists. It seems easy to dismiss the feelings and wants of faceless future tourists who would only be passing through the Burren. Siting a center just to facilitate the taking of snapshots and the bringing home of souvenirs of Mullaghmore from the center's shop seems practically a crime, pandering to the dollar and the deutsche mark at the risk of destroying the Burren itself.

But as we live in Clare, we are not so sure. Tourism *is* the largest industry in the country. There *is* an urgent need for any kind of jobs to employ people here. The strongest voices in favor of the proposed center are all local. And the speakers are as eager for the center to be built at Mullaghmore as they are passionate in declaring their love for the Burren. They are trying to make a living here, in a sparsely populated corner of the country. Are theirs the voices to heed? Does the west of Ireland exist nowadays for tourists? The resolution of this issue will tell us a lot about ourselves, and Ireland's future. This controversy is not as absurd as it might have seemed to me ten years ago for, increasingly, it is the tourism industry in the brief summers that keeps small coastal villages alive. Where can the students in my graduating class look for work? They will circulate in May among the small restaurants and cafés in Kilkee and Lahinch, and ask for jobs in hotels that hug the coast and circle the Burren. Families living in the West must come up with new ideas to keep their incomes from falling to the point where a moderate living can no longer be eked out here. As farm incomes have dropped and rearing cattle in competition with the rest of Europe has become nonviable, the Irish Farmers' Association itself has been pushing for farmers to try the alternative of farm tourism. It is the people living *in* the Burren who need the jobs. And while a center in Corofin would be environmentally friendly, it would benefit least those who need it the most. Our resource is the landscape; the decision of how to use it will determine who will live here.

In December, diggers began excavating the Mullaghmore site. There were protests and marches in Dublin, though much of the money for the development was coming from the rest of Europe, and it was said that if work did not begin before the year's end it could be withdrawn altogether.

Then in January 1993, in the aftermath of the general election, Dick Spring decided to lead the Labor Party into a coalition government with Fianna Fail. This coalition was, on the face of it, quite remarkable. The parties had seemed to be opposites. Uneasiness grew; what change would result from this?

Prior to the election, Labor had declared itself opposed to the Mullaghmore building site; Fianna Fail had been in favor of it. In the first hundred days of the new government coalition, this was the issue that threatened to sunder it. The Labor minister, Michael D. Higgins (a Galway man and a poet, now in charge of arts, cultural affairs, and the Gaeltachts), flew over the mountain in a helicopter—and suggested moving the center elsewhere. Dr. Bhamjee, his new colleague in government, our representative, spoke softly of finding a solution to please everybody. His responses seemed calm and studied in a way that set him apart from the rest of the politicians in the House. Then the Burren Action Group brought a legal action for an injunction in the high court against the Office of Public Works on the grounds, novel in Ireland, that the OPW had never applied for planning permission for the center. Simply because it was a government body did not, said the court, absolve it from the obligation of seeking planning permission. For the time being, the diggers have stopped. The delay will allow for another round of discussion and reappraisal, but the Mullaghmore issue is being faced around the globe: the environment versus jobs.

Like many other towns and villages in the West, Kilmihil has seen enormous change in the past few decades; the village that once centered around the church, the local fair, and the creamery is very different now. In 1978 the cattle mart replaced the old fair days when animals were sold on the main street of Kilmihil. But today the mart has largely fallen into disuse. Cattle are now brought twenty miles to Ennis or fifteen miles into Kilrush instead. Farmers bring their milk into the village only to meet the creamery trailer, which arrives in Kilmihil three days a week, takes the milk from the farmers' bulk tanks, and heads off to other rural villages down the road, before bringing the milk to a central point in Tipperary. When we arrived in the village almost ten years ago, there were five grocery shops. Now there are three. Sean Fitzpatrick's pub has closed. Of the five other pubs in the village, three carry on secondary businesses, like the butcher shop run by Helena Ryan or the tile shop adjoining Daly's Lounge. Among the pubs business is brisk only on weekends when college students return by bus and the village's population briefly swells. The increase in the price of a pint and the relative scarcity of money have meant that on most evenings it is only in the last hours before closing that the customers come in. For a time there was a shoe shop in the village, but it closed, for the days when all shopping was done in the parish are gone, and the sales and variety of choice in Ennis and Kilrush hard to beat. Lernihan's grocery shop has turned into a video store, open only at night. On the other hand, Johnston's has developed from a small grocer's into a large supermarket-hardware-feed store. When his father retired, Gerry Johnston, a married man not yet forty with four young children and a two-story house across the street from the shop, took over. He is now a leading business-man in the village. Johnston's supermarket draws customers from all the outlying townlands of Kilmihil Parish and beyond. It advertises on Clare FM, the local radio station broadcasting from Ennis, and in the *Clare Champion,* our newspaper, and its sales draw people from villages within a ten-mile radius. We, too, shop more frequently in Kilmihil than in Ennis now, but still must go to Ennis to get those things for which there seems no demand in a rural village: ground coffee or Parmesan cheese or black olives.

Deirdre ought to have ballet lessons, I thought. She has grown from a chubby baby into a slender girl with long straight legs. She is graceful and erect and holds her head high. She loves the idea of ballet: the look and the music of ballet, and the clothes. At five, our Deirdre is very fashion conscious. But even more compelling is my wish that Deirdre have something special that is all her own. Because she is our adopted daughter she is already set apart from the other children here. And the fact that Niall and I are not "like" the other parents seems to add to her separateness.

Almost everyone in Deirdre's school comes from a farming family (with the exception of her friend Vanessa). Her two other closest friends are Una and Colette Downes, also farm children, but the younger of the Downes girls is three years older than Deirdre. There are only six other children in her grade at school and no one her age within walking distance of us. There are no after school activities for the children and so her afternoons are spent in the house with me and playing with Joseph. It is one of the drawbacks of rural life.

Sometimes it does strike me as absurd that we live in the

heart of rural, farming Ireland since we do not farm ourselves now. Our needs as a family, our aspirations for ourselves and our children are sometimes considerably
different from our neighbors' and our friends'. We are accepted as being "the ones who write the books," or "the one
who does the pictures," and Deirdre as our daughter is
accepted as well. But even though the community accepts
us, it makes a distinction. Deirdre senses this; it is an issue
that needs addressing.

At first I adapted to the rural way of life more readily than
I do at the moment. Now I sometimes tire of it. (But I tired of
commuting, too.) For thirty years Westchester County, New
York, was my home. And while I have lived here almost ten
years I will never be *from* here, not in the way others are. I
want Deirdre and Joseph to be exposed to the kind of cultural opportunities that are rare here in Kilmihil. I will give
them what I can, certain, too, that growing up here in the
countryside offers its special opportunities as well.

They will never have what American kids have, but neither will they be faced with the same fears and dangers that
are becoming increasingly a part of American childhood.

So I am happy to travel thirty minutes to Ennis to take
Deirdre to ballet classes. The fact that ballet classes of a very
high standard are actually offered in Ennis is, of course,
wonderful, and a comment on the changing West. So I go,
not only to give her an opportunity but also because when
she grows older I want her to be able to say, Yes, I am
different, not because I am adopted, but because in the
house where I grew up there were books everywhere, and
drawings, and paintings on the wall. There was Thanksgiv-
ing in November and Christmases in America, and Daddy's

plays at the Abbey Theatre, and there were ballet lessons and set dancing lessons, and we had a horse and a donkey and a cat and a hen in the garden. . . .

One night, sitting across the open hearth from me after the children were in bed, Chris said, "If we are going to live here, we can't *just* live here or we might as well have a house in Galway or Ennis. We've chosen to live in a rural community and to bring up children in the countryside. There's no point to our living in Kiltumper if we're not going to live in Kilmihil, too."

We don't want Kilmihil to become just a place we pass through on our way into Ennis. So, that night, in a determined mood, we decided to try and become more involved.

I do not mean to suggest that the village had become dormant. Indeed, in Kilmihil on any given night, you might find the keep-fit group jumping about in Larry's new gym at the school, or a prayer meeting in a classroom, or the ladies of the Kilmihil branch of the Irish Countrywomen's Association at a lecture on heart disease, or the Apostolic Works people sewing and embroidering religious garments for the missions, or our parish priest himself, Father Malone, instructing a bridge class. Rather, it was we who felt the need of a community. It was our own sense that the four-o'clock darkness that swept in across Hayes' Hill and the valley could easily maroon us in the cottage night after night. Now that we had really settled into life here we had less time to go on the *cuaird*, visiting neighbors. And people who knew us well enough to drop by often assumed we were too busy. Life with small children had curtailed our sociability as had the demands of self-employment. But we had come here in search of a community to belong to, and before the children came, we had begun to take our places in it. Now it was time to make another effort.

There had been no production from the Kilmihil Drama Group the previous year, and so at this year's meeting I offered to direct *The Chastitute* by John B. Keane. A week later I put a note in the parish newsletter, which was distributed at mass, saying French classes for adults would begin in the school on Monday nights. And I joined the Tidy Towns Committee.

The Tidy Towns Competition is a national event organized through the tourist board to try and promote a greater awareness of cleanliness, tidiness, and the general appearance of towns and villages throughout the country. Sometime during the early summer an adjudicator would make a surprise visit to inspect the roads for litter, the shopfronts for fresh paint, and to note amenities, developments, and general improvements of any kind. Some months later our local Tidy Towns Committee would receive the report with a grade bestowed for its efforts. Several categories were judged and a number of prizes awarded annually. The most coveted prize was the award for the tidiest town in Ireland. We are not in that category. Kilmihil's goal is to simply improve over last year's mark, to try to encourage pride of place.

The committee meeting was held in the secondary school on a Monday night at eight o'clock. Larry's philosophy as the school's principal is that the facilities it offers should be available to all the community—"No problem"—so most evenings groups and organizations gather there. I arrived early and received a warm welcome from Paddy and Maura Cotter. The Cotters, a Kilmihil couple in their late fifties who live just outside the village, are selflessly interested in improving the community. A big man with a quick laugh, Paddy teaches woodworking in Kilrush. He's handy with a hammer and "tasty" with a brush, as they say, and his handmade signs depicting the village and offering a welcome in Gaelic stand at each of the four entrances to Kilmihil. Maura, tiny in comparison to Paddy, is a retired school teacher and mother of seven grown children. She is the secretary of the Kilmihil Tidy Towns Committee, and as we waited for others to arrive, she handed me last year's report. In it, the adjudicator had criticized the derelict state of a number of buildings in the village, noted that some of the grass areas were unplanted, and observed that we needed an overall plan.

Michael Fitzpatrick, the young owner of the petrol station and grocery at the head of the village, and Gregory Fitzgerald, the village postmaster and chairman of the committee, arrived followed soon afterwards by Joe Sullivan, a local builder, as well as Larry and Father Malone.

Father Malone has been in the parish only a few years. He is from Miltown Malbay, ten miles up the coast, a man of sixty, tall and erect with thinning silver hair. He, too, was a teacher, retired now from St. Flannan's in Ennis. He walks with a quick kind of a shuffle and enters a room with his shoulders squared and his hands in his jacket pockets. He is usually wearing his Lahinch Golf Club sweater vest. It was because of his urging that Kilmihil now has a golf society whose members play regularly at the Kilrush Golf Club.

Indeed, he is often teased that his true vocation is to convert unbelievers—to bridge and golf. He is both shy and reserved but can voice his opinion strongly when the need arises. Like us, Father Malone is trying to belong to the community and offers his skills apart from those of his calling. In the evening he can sometimes be found down at Kirk's pub enjoying a glass of vodka.

"Is this all there is?" I asked, surveying the other seven present.

"This is a good crowd, sure," came back the mocking reply.

We sat in the bright room where earlier in the day I had taught a French class to sixteen teenagers. In all the meetings I have attended in Clare, there is a kind of preamble before the main event. Nothing starts quite on time, and the sitting around and light chat seem as much a part of the meeting as the business itself. The talk goes carefully around the edge of the subject at hand—and sometimes disappears down a long winding road of its own.

Paddy Cotter is particularly gifted at this. He finds humor in everything and particularly, it seems, in disasters. This is typically Irish, I think, a way of dealing with failure and loss. At its best, humor enables us to keep going; at its worst, it turns cynical and negative. Humor was at its best at our meeting that night.

"You're doing another play this year?" Paddy asked me. "Good man." And with that he began to chuckle. "Do you remember that time in Waterford? Jeepers."

"The All-Ireland Final."

"That's right."

"*The Man Who Wouldn't Go to Heaven.*"

"I remember that one," said Larry. "We had to make Paddy an angel costume."

"He was some angel all right," Maura laughed, thinking of her large husband, bare-legged, in a knee-length gown of white satin, a white posy on his head.

"He had to start the show," I explained. "I put on a record of Fred Astaire singing 'I'm in Heaven' and as the curtain opened Paddy was to dance out in his costume."

Paddy shook his head, remembering himself. "And on the night, just before we were to start, do you see, I said to myself I'll pop into the bathroom. It was down below the stage. So off I popped in my angel rigout and the next thing, I turned around and wasn't the flaming door stuck . . ."

"I'd switched on the music," I said.

"And I pulled the curtain," said Larry.

Paddy could hardly get out the words, he was so amused at one of the greatest disasters of the Kilmihil Drama Group— and at the All-Ireland Finals, no less. ". . . And I could hear Fred Astaire singing, 'I'm in heaven, I'm in heaven,' while I was locked in below, shouting, 'I'm in the toilet, I'm in the toilet!!' O cripes!!"

About half an hour later Gregory opened the meeting. "And we welcome new faces," he said in a wry monotone voice that mixed dismay with humor. The report was read out. What could be done? There had been an improvement last year of three points: window boxes and hanging baskets had been nicely filled; a couple of wrought-iron seats placed outside shops; and storefronts had been painted (although Chris found the colors still too muted, too many nondescript beiges that flowed together when you drove through the village).

Throughout the meeting, as the talk went on, I was struck by the continued efforts of these people on behalf of their community in the face of what seemed to be little support from the greater part of the population. They worked on regardless.

"We must pick things that we can get done. Nothing too ambitious, you know. I'd be happy if we just dealt with some of the things that we know we can manage first," said Gregory."

"Lacken Road is a disgrace," said Joe Sullivan, an energetic young man. "You come into the village and what do you see? Only old plastic bags and bits of rubbish all along the ditches. It's a disgrace, so it is." Many's the time he had tidied it up himself.

There was a lengthy pause.

"Right," said Gregory. "Well, let's attack that one. What about organizing a cleanup along the Lacken Road?"

It was set for the following Monday evening at five-thirty.

On Monday evening the sky was overcast, but not raining. The weather stayed dry and the little breeze was warm. On the Lacken Road the rubbish waited—flecked green, yellow, and black bits, wire, containers, wrappings, bottles, stuff that had found its way into the ditch. Joe Sullivan arrived with his trailer; Paddy Cotter was there. And we carried on, quietly pulling stuff from the hedgerows and filling our bags, tidying the village even though only a handful of people came and the rain was close behind them.

Monday, Wednesday, and Friday evenings the breadman comes. P. J. Coote heads out from his family-run bakery in

Ennis at midday and drives along the quiet back roads of the townlands with a van full of everything. He and John Cassidy, his assistant, bring more than bread. They bring news, they bring contact, and in many households theirs may be the only knock on the door that day. They know everybody. In the back of the van they carry everything from bartered cabbages to duck eggs and maybe a fresh trout in season, from a bag of Taytos for Deirdre to a chocolate bar for Chris, an apple for Joseph, and a can of Coke for me. Butter and cream and rashers and eggs and sausages, and to our house, they bring something extra as well. They bring chess.

During the years in Kilmihil I have never managed to find someone with whom to regularly indulge one of the passions of my youth, chess. Then one evening, John, the twenty-year-old helper in the bread van, mentioned he wouldn't be here on Friday, he was going to Kilkenny to play in the championships.

"What championships?" I asked him.

"Chess," he said. "I have to defend my title."

And so began our series of marathon matches on Mondays, Wednesdays, and Fridays. They became a ritual. I set up the board in the new kitchen and waited as the winter darkness closed in for the sound of the bread van. Between half past six and seven o'clock, depending on the weather and business, the van lights would blaze down the Kiltumper road. Two hoots would announce its arrival in the driveway. While P. J. turned the van around, John would rush in, a loaf of warm bread under his arm.

"My move is it, Mr. Williams?" he'd ask.

He'd slide the bread onto the counter and bend down over the board. In the minute or two he had to make his move before P. J. hooted and he had to run out again, his eyes didn't flicker. They were fixed on the board with such concentration that you could almost sense the myriad permutations of possible moves clicking through his mind at high speed. Watching him, I remembered the passion with which I played chess when I was a teenager. I had two days to make my move; John, less than two minutes for his. He had no duplicate board nor any record other than in his mind of where the game stood. But he is a champion; he lives and dreams chess to the exclusion of all else. He has beaten everyone in Munster his age.

Deirdre and Joseph would stand by in the kitchen, watching. They could see nothing but they felt something in this strangely powerful, concentrated moment in the winter nighttime.

The van might hoot as John moved his bishop. "See you Friday, Mr. Williams."

And John Cassidy would be off to make his deliveries through the countryside, this secret chess player breadman. After ten games, played over three months, I have yet to beat him.

It was six o'clock in the evening, the children were in their pajamas, and we were playing a game of pretend monsters in the dark in the new kitchen. Chris was sitting with her coffee by the big fire, trying to read as Joseph came running at alarming speed, to throw himself face first against the upheld newspaper.

"Monsters! Monsters!" he shouted, moments before Deirdre in her long white "bride's" nightdress came rushing along behind him, screaming about the demons at her heels. "Monsters, Joseph, monsters! Aaahh!!"

I was in mid-monster when the phone rang, and the children were still screaming as I picked up the receiver.

It was Garry Hynes.

"Listen, Niall," she said. "I've read the new play and I think it's terrific."

"Monsters are coming, Joseph! Watch out!!" Both children ran across the room and grabbed me by the leg.

". . . So," Garry continued, "I'll have a contract sent down to you next week, okay?"

"Aaaaaghghghgh!" Joseph took off, running and roaring into the new kitchen pursued by Deirdre—and then Chris and me, too, all of us racing around the new room, playing and shouting, now the happiest monsters ever.

✦ Four ✦

Water, water, everywhere. In a place where it rains so much, plenitude and purity of water seem the least to expect. Our own water comes from a spring-fed well in a field called the Grove next to the house. It has been there longer than living memory, for at least the two hundred years the present house has stood. Even in houses on the other side of the parish Chris and I have heard comments about it: "Johnny Breen's was a lovely well, so it was. There was always a jam jar next to it there in the bush. I often remember going in that field for a glass. That was lovely water there." And, although our great friend Mary Breen has clean running water in her house down the road, every day her brother-in-law Joeso Breen still comes back along the Kiltumper road with two orange plastic buckets to fill from the well because it is, simply, the best water around. The spring well in the grove is a blessing to us. That it has never run dry is another reason for its celebrity.

A submerged circle of stones in a tangle of woodbine and ivy, bracken and bramble, the well is little more than a hole in the ground with a battered sheet of corrugated iron thrown up against it. Our electric pump stands just beside the spring and brings the water into the house.

But in February the family was struck by a series of stomachaches. The children had faint cramps that came and went. Chris, hearing about a service in Ennis, decided to get the water checked. It was not something I would normally have done: Many of the houses around had spring-fed wells of their own, and certainly very few of their wells had ever been checked or analyzed; it simply wasn't an Irish thing to do. If the water ran clear through the tap and tasted fine, as ours did, you thanked God and left it alone. But with the children complaining of stomach pains, there was, I agreed, no harm in checking. After all, didn't everyone know we had the finest water around?

A little embarrassed that we were committing a kind of local sacrilege by even thinking of having the well tested, I didn't tell Mary Breen or Michael Downes or our other neighbors. I waited for the results to come from the Midwestern Health Board, certain of what they would say.

I came home from school one afternoon to find Chris sitting at the window looking out on the rain-swept garden.

"Do you want the bad news or the bad news?" she said. "The results of the water test came back, they just phoned."

"Well?"

"We can't drink the water. It's unfit for human consumption."

"What's the matter with it?" I asked, thinking this was just bureaucracy, this was "European standards" and probably something to do with fluoride levels for teeth or something.

"It has fifty-five different forms of *coli* in it."

"What?"

"And Council water, furnished by the authorities, is only allowed to have five. We have *fifty*-five." She sighed and looked away out into the rain. "God, Niall, what are we going to do?"

Suddenly the blessing had been taken away. Day after day, the skies poured with rain, water puddled the fields, and we seemed to be living in a very waterland. The water came through the taps perfectly clear and insidiously sparkling, but we couldn't drink it. Immediately, we went on bottled water. I had P. J. Crowley, who is also our postman, come on a Saturday with his digger and deepen and refill with stones the soakage pit off the septic tank. It was unlikely to be the source of the contamination but we had to be doing something. And then, one afternoon, Michael Downes came up, bringing our new neighbor Jim Channon with him for a look.

In the time that we have been in Kiltumper, Michael's farm has tripled in size, and he has a reputation of being a shrewd yet careful man. He's a short man in big Wellingtons, a cap never off his head, and a cigarette about to go out or about to be lit in his hand. Over the years Michael has given us more advice than has anyone else, and more times than not we have followed it. Recently, Michael sold the empty cottage on a farm he had bought to Jim and Kay Channon, the newest arrivals in the townland. As he had when we arrived, Michael made them feel welcome by including them.

Jim is an Englishman in his late fifties. He grew up on a farm in Devon where everything was run in a perfectly ordered English way, and as a result he often finds the West Clare way of farming verging on the comically absurd. After a varied life in different corners of the world, most recently in the London Ambulance Service, Jim had decided to retire to a cottage in the west of Ireland. He loves the scenic beauty of Kerry especially, and there, a few years ago, he met and married his "Kerry girl," Kay. A charming and warm woman in her forties with a thick head of curls and laughing eyes, Kay is the perfect foil to Jim's English reserve. Conversations between them are often nationalist in tone; Jim all "The way we do it in England" and Kay, in her musical Kerry accent, "Well, you're in Ireland now, Jim."

They had arrived in Kilmihil by fluke really, coming up one Sunday from the Killimer ferry, which brings tourists from Kerry. They immediately liked the tranquillity of Kilmihil and inquired about a house. Now they are completely settled in the old cottage at the top of the hill, a two-mile walk from us. Jim is an experienced handyman and Kay, a seamstress and decorator. Between them they have converted the cottage into a warm old-style home with a glass conservatory all along the front. Both of them are keen gardeners.

Now, with Jim, the six-foot-tall Englishman on one side of me and Michael, short, with smoke rising from under his cap, on the other, I crossed into the Grove and walked to the well to view the problem firsthand. Michael could not simply witness a problem, he'd have to suggest something.

"I haven't been here in years, you know, Niall," he said, "but at one time I was in here a lot. When I was a young lad there were apple trees."

Now there were brambles. Stepping through them I could feel Jim's amazement that in here, somewhere, was our water source. His own was a covered well within a shed. We walked along a mucky track and stood looking down at the well, the sunken ring of stones with the rusted corrugated iron resting against it. The stones themselves were covered in moss, there were ferns growing in the crevices, and little lumps of mud and leaf mulch. It appeared romantic and picturesque, and a bit archaic.

Michael hummed a little tune to himself and kicked with his Wellington at the overgrowth above the well. "Oh yes," he said to himself. "Oh yes." He kicked a little clearing with his boot, then stood back and took out a new cigarette. "Not great, Jim," he said.

"No, Michael. Needs a little maintenance," said Jim.

Michael spoke through a smoke cloud, his right eye half-shut. "There was a drain above that well one time, Niall," he said, and I remembered Mary Breen telling me the same thing once. I had done nothing about it. I couldn't see any sign of a drain now. The whole place was a tangle of overgrowth, of luxuriant ivy and woodbine falling over the well.

There's your problem, I'd say, Niall," said Michael. "Sure, that well hasn't been cleaned out in years. Did you ever teem it?"

"No."

He slowly nodded and hummed a bit of the tune before

coming back to the conversation. "Well, that's the first order of business, I'd say. What would you say, Jim?"

"Well yes, I'd say so. Certainly."

"And cut away all that old stuff that's growing up around it. Right?"

They went away again on Michael's tractor, leaving me their advice. Bending down under the flagstone and into the well, I felt deeply ashamed. It was such a simple thing to do: Clean the well. I began washing off the stones, pulling away the ferns, and pelting bucket after bucket of water out behind me, feeling very guilty. I had let the clearest springwater for miles around become tainted and polluted until my whole family was getting sick. I had become too far removed from the land, I realized, too much the teacher in the schoolroom, too bookish, lost in the classroom and the writing of books and plays in the little garret room upstairs. What else did I need to remind me, to call me back, than this fouled water I bucketed out of the well with growing fury at myself? It was my fault. A few years earlier, I told myself, this would never have happened. I was more in touch then. I would have noticed the woodbine and the bramble overtaking the source, would have been more intimate with the place around me. How complacent I had become, filling my glass of water from the tap without another thought, like a city dweller. There and then I swore I would be a better caretaker of the land, would not take for granted this water, these hill fields and meadows, ditches and drains.

I bent and dipped and flung the water back behind me again and again while a dark drenched stain spread on my left shoulder.

As it happened, the water itself did not contain any forms

of *E. coli*, only fifty-five forms of vegetation and perhaps some animal life. We learned this when the written report came in the post some days later, and felt a bit better. Now our refreshed and teemed spring well is back in the water business.

I'm beginning to see daffodil leaf tips springing up all over, but in all the wrong places. We reorganized the front border and moved it back to make a wider path in front of the cottage but we forgot to move the daffodils last summer. Now they are coming up through the sandstone gravel—which is nice, too, but will make it a bit dodgy for walking, I think. The "daffs" I did remember to transplant to the slope in the haggard near the haybarn are sprouting. That's where daffodils belong—in the wild. Several years of gardening have taught me that. Then they can die back naturally without disgracing themselves. Now, we only have to keep the donkey away from them.

The Chastitute is a dirty play. Or so I heard two days after announcing that I would direct it this year for the Kilmihil Drama Group. It was enough to break your heart, if you let it. Like everything else in a small, rural place there are equal measures of hesitation and excitement in doing something new. And *The Chastitute* was going to be new. Even the title was enough to grab attention and stir either uncertainty or anticipation, depending with whom you spoke.

It is one of John B. Keane's less-produced works. It tells the story of a bachelor farmer who relives his many pathetic and hilarious attempts to find a woman, moving from a scene in a brothel in Cork to the confessional to a kitchen in Kerry to the Spring Show in Dublin and back again. I figured it was the perfect vehicle to get the drama group back on the road after a year's lapse. For this, I partly blamed myself, for having been too caught up in the Dublin theater, "real" theater. But drama was real in Kilmihil, too, and perhaps more important to the community here. I had the feeling that if no play were done this year, then the group could easily melt away, ending an almost unbroken sixty-year tradition of amateur drama in the village.

In late September the cast of twelve had begun to meet in the assembly hall of the school one or two nights a week. Since I had last directed the group, I had become a professional playwright, and now I was keenly aware both of a sense of expectation from the players and my own wish to give back to Kilmihil everything I knew or had recently learned about theater.

We first read the play in a light, laughing, easy way with people stopping and starting, reacting to each other's lines as we sat around the airy hall with hailstones battering against the glass. But when our leading actor, David O'Connell, who works at a school in Ennis, read the principal role of John

Bosco, with Joe Hassett, the milkman from Cooraclare, as Mickey Molly the Matchmaker, come to note down his preferences in females, you could sense the actors slipping into character. The bare room, with the seats up on the tables for the following morning's school, became a bachelor farmer's country kitchen. Language was all it was about; there were no props and no movement yet, we were only beginning, and still you could feel the magic, the transforming quality of it that impressed me more than even the morning I came into the Abbey through the front doors to see the set of my own play on the stage.

Gerry Harty, a close friend married to Kilmihil's only doctor, and as elegant a young mother as ever there was, was the Cork lady of the night. Michael Mescall, a tall, red-bearded water engineer, in Father Malone's second suit, was the priest; Lucy, Pat, Tommy, Jude, Kathleen, Gertie, and David's wife, Pat O'Connell, doubling roles as they read the scenes, became the people around John Bosco, all of whom were steadily ruining his life.

It is a funny and sad play; a play written in anger at the ways visiting missionaries, sermonizing and preaching repentance, drilled a kind of terror of sexuality into the soul of the bachelor; how the mystique surrounding the female in his society brought John Bosco to a life of impossible loneliness and pain. There are scenes in it of great comedy swiftly followed by moments of pathos and despair. In reading the play, I had felt it belonged to an earlier time. It wasn't simply that the text was twelve years old; it was no longer true in rural Ireland that missionaries arriving each year during Lent could strike terror in a parish. The secondary schoolchildren

I came across every day were far from being terrorized by the church. Indeed, they were far more at ease with the opposite sex than I had been at that age.

Midway through rehearsals I began to wonder whom the play would speak to. Was it too dated? Would the whole thing flop or perhaps be seen as an attempt by someone who had never experienced the missions to make fun of something the village remembered as valid and alive?

By January the cast had learned the lines for three-quarters of the play. They had been given movements and we had used seats and benches for the various locations. They pantomimed when they were without props: "Then I go over here and get a glass and the bottle from here, right?" And it was all going fine until someone finally asked, "She's not really going to take off her clothes, is she?"

For weeks Gerry had mimed the actions: She was in her bedroom with John Bosco, he gave her a drink, she asked him to undo her back buttons, he gave her another drink, she asked him to help pull her slip over her head, he gave her another drink. She staggered into the bed. He undressed down to his longjohns, gargled with whiskey, and approached the bed in a great tangle of anticipation and terror. And found her asleep. End of scene.

Of course she was going to take her clothes off. She knew it. I knew it. I thought we all knew it. I said yes, when asked the question, and got a quiet "I see" for an answer. For days afterwards I was unnerved. Maybe I was pushing the whole thing too much, maybe I was imposing an outside morality, an outsider's view of things on the group. I had already agreed with Chris that the backdrop for the play would be a large mural of female figures; a tableau of women, nudes, nuns, prostitutes, and mothers rising vaguely out of the ground. They were the figures haunting Bosco's imagination, I felt, and were appropriate, as the whole play took place in his memory on the night he was about to commit suicide for want of love. Chris had begun on the scale drawing, but at the rehearsal that week when one of our actresses asked me in a very forthright way what the background was going to be, I just said we were working on it.

The closer we got to the first performance, the less sure I was about the show. And the cast became ever more jittery. There were phone calls and visits to the house. Joe stopped by regularly and chain-smoked up the chimney.

"Tell me again now how you see Mickey Molly, will you? Because I don't want to get it wrong. I don't have him at all yet, I'd say, do I?"

"Oh, you do, Joe."

"No no, I don't feel I do now, and damn it, it's bad enough that I came looking for a part and I'm only letting you down." Joe is a chronic worrier. His short red-freckled fingers are yellowed from smoke and his voice has become gravelly and soft. He and his wife, Mary, have a dozen children. And he suited the part of the matchmaker perfectly.

"You're one of the best things in it."

"Arrah cripes no, no, I'd just like to get it right, do you see?"

The phone rings. It's David O'Connell, our John Bosco.

"I think it needs a lot of work still, Niall."

"It doesn't, David, it's not too bad at all now."

"I don't feel I have him quite right."

"Why don't you come up and we'll talk it through."

"Okay, Niall, I'll be there in ten minutes."

The following morning I met Gertie, who played John Bosco's stern housekeeper, in Ennis. She didn't beat around the bush.

"We're on in a week, Niall."

"Yes."

"We won't be ready."

"Of course we will."

"Not a chance of it, Niall. I don't think we'll be ready in three weeks."

Meanwhile, in the village shops I kept meeting with anticipation. "The play'll be on soon, Niall."

"It will."

"I hear it's very funny."

"It is," I said, losing all conviction and wandering out into the daylight ever more unsure of what we had gotten ourselves into.

In the middle of the week we made the move from the school assembly hall to the stage in the community center. At the back of the hall, facing the stage, a couple of teenagers were playing badminton. The actors came and went across the small stage, saying their lines, their voices lost beneath the loud whacks and eager cries of the badminton players. They looked down uncertainly at me. A few visitors stopped by and stood at the side looking on. None of them laughed before drifting off into the night.

The first act, in rehearsal, took two hours. I had invited Father Malone to see the show in case he found anything objectionable, but he came and left the dreadful rehearsal, his hands in his jacket pockets, giving me just a nod. I supposed he was leaving things to me. Still, we ploughed on. The badminton players finished and came to the stage to watch, but even the free show didn't hold them for long.

At a quarter to one in the morning I locked the community hall doors behind me and went home to Chris. It was too late to stop now. I couldn't tell the cast I was unsure about the whole thing; couldn't cancel the performances in Kilmihil or the tour to the festivals in Doonbeg, Scariff, and Claregalway. The following morning Chris began work on the backdrop mural. It was still a wash of pale blue undercoat when the cast came in that night. Nobody said a word, but the following morning when I met one of them, he said: "Somebody was saying, Niall, that blue is very poor on stage. It reflects the light badly or something. You never use blue."

"That's only the undercoat," I said shortly.

"Oh, is it? Right," he said.

"Right," said I and turned quickly on my heel, heading off to the hall where Chris had begun to paint the women's figures. As in earlier years, Chris had been called upon to whip up a set with Larry Blake, our consummate stage manager. Larry, Chris feels, would love to be on stage himself if only he could remember lines and if only his wife, Lucy, one of our leading ladies, would let him. And Larry partly believes the same about Chris. The truth is that together they are happier being behind the scenes. And between Chris's artistic sense and Larry's know-how they manage to bang together a fine set. This year Deirdre is helping Chris and holds her paintbrush just like her mother. It is easy to see how in a rural village whole families can be gradually drawn into some passion, whether it is the football team, the athletics club, or in our case, the drama group. In another couple of years I can imagine Joseph as well down in the hall on cold February days sponging and dripping paint under his mother's joyful eye.

Tuesday night was the first performance. ("Tuesday's a bad night for plays. You mightn't get too many to come.") Because the church across the street was still being renovated, the hall was filled with the church pews, and the altar table and crucifix and candles had to be taken off the stage. But in the space of an hour or so, the church became the theater. The kitchen range was brought on, the bar, the bed, the brothel, and the baby Ford. By the time darkness was falling it was ready, and Chris and I stood at the front of the stage, nervously looking down at the empty pews.

Chris and Gerard Finucane, who always gets called upon to help with the lights and who always reluctantly but good-naturedly agrees, were cueing the lights; the Cotters, Paddy and Maura were at the door; Larry was hovering up and down. In a room to the side that served as both the credit union office and the small chapel during the church renovations, the cast was getting dressed and made up.

Lucy had her script in hand. David was sitting staring out of darkly aged eyes with Joe bent over him graying his hair. Michael Mescall was coming and going, blessing us, in Father's soutane and hat. Each of them glanced at me as I came in the door, asking for assurance.

"Is there anyone out there, Niall?"

"There is," I lied. "They're coming in now," I said, standing before the door so that no one might look out and see that with fifteen minutes to the announced curtain time there were less than a dozen people in the hall. What if they didn't come? Would the lapse of a year have weakened the interest of our audience in going out on a wintry Tuesday night to see a show? Or had television eaten that bit further into the audience? Was this another sign of change? Or, worse, of resistance to it? Had the word gone ahead of us: This is a dirty play?

As I stood inside the door watching the cast, giving last-minute reminders and saying the little nervous, needless things you say when you know you are about to lose control, I was listening for the sounds of an audience outside. Half past eight came and went.

"We'll give them a few more minutes to get their seats," I announced.

Father Malone slipped in the door as Michael Mescall was about to bless me.

"Good luck to ye. It'll go very well."

"Thank you, Father."

"Right so."

And as he turned, someone asked, "Father, is there anyone . . .?"

He looked back at the cast with a smile. "Packed," he said, "and waiting for you. Good luck now."

Then there was the rush from the side room across the corridor, the cast like fragile spirits in their costumes flitting across, trying to avoid the bad luck of being seen before their entrances. The last good lucks were said, and the cast took up cramped positions in the tiny wings. A general murmur, shrieks from the children, announcements—ready music, ready curtain, ready lights—and then, to the sound of a John McCormack recording of "I Dream of Jeannie," I pulled the curtain slowly, the lights came up on the gigantic female figures on the backdrop, and the show opened.

It was a moment of validation of our choice of life. From the time the first speeches began to draw the crowd into the world of the play, there was deep satisfaction. They were laughing, there was warmth and generosity throughout the hall, and the more it came, this gratitude and appreciation of skill and effort, the more the actors responded. By the time Gerry appeared in the Cork brothel with John Bosco, his timid eyes, and his full bottle of vodka, the audience was ready for anything, I thought. Swaying and slurring, she asked him to unbutton her dress. And the simplest flick of his fingers in the air like a master safecracker, the screwing-up of his eyes, had the audience in the church pews roaring and shushing each other to hear more.

Right then, we didn't know the play would find the same response wherever it went, that the hall in Doonbeg would be packed so tightly the following night you could walk on heads to the back door and out to the toilets, with people peering over each other's shoulders to see. We didn't know that it would win the award of Most Entertaining Play in the festival, and do the same in Claregalway, where David would win Best Actor, or that we would bring it back to Kilmihil two weeks later and fill the hall again down into the badminton court with people cramming in to see it. We didn't know it would be the most popular play in many years. But it didn't really matter. For in the hall that night there was simple proof that a living tradition linked our performance with all the men and women of the village down the decades who had crossed that stage and become for their own people the night's stars. By the time I pulled the curtain closed on the tableau of the cast standing with their rosary beads, seeming to blend and fade into the painting of nudes, nuns, and ladies of the night, with John McCormack singing softly once more, even the roar and applause of that audience had become one with all the others. The place was alive with a feeling of community and warmth. And it felt good.

⚜ FIVE ⚜

There are four national schools in our parish, and among them ten teachers and 130 children. Deirdre went to Clonigulane, a two-room, two-teacher schoolhouse a mile and a half up the straight road from us on the boggy hillside. The cream-colored school stands on its own surrounded by an old stone wall and acres of bog and sky. Not a single tree shelters the children from winter's westerly winds but they don't seem to mind a bit. Chris and Joseph can hear their crisp laughter as it is carried on the wind down to our front garden, and we know that Deirdre is safe and happy within the walls of the hundred-year-old schoolhouse.

Yvonne Callinan, a young married mother herself, is Deirdre's teacher, and Kieran Cleary is the school's second teacher and principal. Yvonne is new to Clonigulane and brings with her the freshness of her youth and enthusiasm. Kieran, a medium-sized man with a lively eye and a diffident manner, has been teaching for almost all his adult life at Clonigulane. He has been principal of the school since 1951, and has taught nine- to twelve-year-old children in the same room for over forty years. Kieran Cleary's life has been his school. His title, the master, is a lingering emblem of respect from the community, carried over from the time when the primary schoolteacher was second in standing only to the village priest. At St. Michael's secondary school I have also encountered the aura of respect that surrounds the primary schoolteacher. Without fail, year after year, a number of the brightest students who might have chosen almost any career give their first option as primary school teaching. The secondary schoolteacher has never acquired that status.

Clonigulane National School was built in 1888 and is one of the oldest buildings still in use in the parish. Only a few years ago the fireplaces were closed up and the turf fires replaced with space heaters. Thirty-six are enrolled, with Mrs. Callinan teaching the junior and senior infants, and first and second class, while Master Cleary teaches the third, fourth, fifth, and sixth classes in the sunny room next door.

When Chris and I first learned of this system we wondered how a teacher could possibly manage. What effect would it have? How could you keep them all quiet and learning? From Dublin I heard stories of my brother Declan's children in classes of thirty-five or forty pupils the same age, all following the same textbooks, and they were doing well.

Now, in Deirdre's room there were eighteen altogether; in her class, there were just six!

Chris drives Deirdre to school at nine-thirty every morning, and collects her again at two when she comes running across the concrete yard with her English reading book, her Irish reading book, and her sums notebook flapping in her bag. From the window of his room Master Cleary sometimes waves.

Within weeks it was obvious that Deirdre was doing well. Her notebooks were filling up and she had made friends. She liked going to school and she liked her teacher. Among her notebooks was one devoted just to news, in which every day the students wrote whatever they had told Mrs. Callinan had happened at home. It was a wonderful thing for us to look at, a record of events as seen through the eyes of the children. Flicking through the pages we read: "Today is Tuesday. Stephen has a new baby brother," or "Michael has two calves," or "Mary has a new blue coat." "Today is Friday. The sun is shining."

Several months after Deirdre began at Clonigulane she came home with a notice of a meeting in the school that evening. By eight o'clock there were thirteen parents crammed into the small desks in the master's room. At the head of the class sat Master Cleary and next to him, Father Malone. Like all national schools, Clonigulane was run by its own board, and Father Malone was its head.

As we waited for the meeting to start, listening for the approach of a car or the creaking of the gate that might herald a latecomer, I looked around at the classroom again. I had been there several times before, mostly to vote in elections, and again was struck by the same thing: the sense of order in that little room. It was a rectangle of learning, the desks set in four rows across the width of the room so the students could gaze up to the master's leather swivel chair. There were two main blackboards at the head of the class. On one of them, in perfectly neat writing in chalk, were a number of Irish verbs in the present tense, three idioms, sample sentences, and more verbs; on the other, columns of figures—all absolutely straight and ordered down the board. Next to these was a large map of the world from after the Second World War—a world pinned against the wall at Clonigulane, temporarily stilled, outside the whirl of change, a world without a Bosnia or Croatia, with the faded pink mass of a single USSR. On the side wall was a picture of the Sacred Heart, and behind the heads of the pupils a framed poster of the 1916 Easter Rising Proclamation next to some EC posters of agriculture in Europe. Nothing about the room was sloppy or haphazard, everything was in its place, and the words on the board bespoke the forty years the master had been there, writing and rubbing chalk off those same boards until it might have seemed to him he was retracing the prints of yesterday's letters onto the ever-erasing face of time itself. Here was a room, I thought, that reflected not an institution, but a man.

The master opened the meeting. Last year a new roof had been needed for the school. This had now been completed, and while a fund-raising dance had been held the previous year, money was still owing for it.

"Now," said the master, pausing and looking down, "there's the desks." He paused again, as if he wished for a moment the problem could be solved just by mentioning it. He made a half-smile. "As you can see, the desks aren't that great. They came, I think, from Leitrim School when they discarded them."

"When was that, Kieran?"

"About 1951, Father."

Amid unabashed laughter, Father smiled. "I see."

We all looked more closely at the desks: double-seated benches on iron stands with chipped-at holes where once the porcelain inkwells had stood for the master to fill from his large bottle of ink. What nibs and spattering and blotting and picking at the neighbor's back they had seen. There had been countless names or initials scratched in all of them. Some had been simply scored and dug at with compass or lead in those moments when the place to be was out in the meadows or going to the mart and not indoors before those twin blackboards.

"So," said the master, his eyes flickering down to the account book before him, his manner becoming ever more diffident as the subject of money loomed, "what would ye think of another social, same as last year, to clear the debt?"

"Well, it was very good last year," said a lady from across the room.

"There wasn't anyone there who didn't have a good time," added Pauline Downes, our neighbor.

"No, no," said the master, "that's right."

"Well, number of tickets, so?" said Father Malone quickly.

"About three hundred, Father, I suppose. Twenty to each family," said the master.

"Right. Price of tickets?"

A pause.

"Three pounds, I suppose, Father."

"Three pounds. Lovely."

"And we'll make a loaf of sandwiches each, same as last year."

The date was set for a fortnight later. The Clonigulane dance to pay off the remaining debt on the new roof would take place at Ryan's Lounge in Kilmihil. Sets of tickets would be given to the pupils in a day or two. The meeting over, we drifted out of the school into the dark.

I was a newcomer to all of this, and, driving home, was learning another lesson about how the school and its community in a rural place were one. It was the school that gave the fields and their houses an identity. The school at the bend in the road beyond the old forge, at the little bridge over the forked river, was the focus for these outlying townlands. In earlier years, before cars shortened the three miles to the center of the village, the people of this place came together in the school. For many of them it had provided their only formal education; their friendships were made here; their children sat in the desks they themselves had sat in; and in many cases so would their children's children. There had been four generations of O'Gormans at Clonigulane, four generations of Downeses.

These school systems in rural places are now threatened. The four schools in the corners of this parish had originally been established a hundred years ago to shorten the distance children had to walk to school. The largest is the village school at Lacken, which still holds four teachers and has close to a hundred pupils. The other three schools, Leitrim, Cahermurphy, and Clonigulane, each have two teachers and are faced with an annual worry that if enrollment drops, the department in Dublin will be forced to downgrade the school to one teacher—with the threat of closing it altogether. From time to time there has been talk in the parish of an amalgamation of the four schools into one centrally located building with buses bringing in the children from the outlying townlands. But this is something the majority of parents do not really want. The added travel time is one negative factor but much deeper is the sense of identity and pride of each of the separate townlands. It is the same everywhere along the west coast of the country; the identity and individuality of different townlands, shaped by the existence of a country school at the side of the road, is in danger of being lost.

Year after year, school enrollment numbers permeate the conversations of our townland. "We're safe for a good few years," our neighbor Kathleen O'Shea told me. And, of course, by moving to Kilmihil and having two children in the school, Chris and I have enlisted in the battle. We don't want our school to go one-teacher, or to close, for the school to be left like so many other deserted buildings as a relic of the old days. From the moment Deirdre started going to the school and bringing home her notebook of "news," we were part of the fight. And if, on a long evening's chat with our friends we might agree that it is inevitable that eventually the local schools will close because the children will simply not be here, it is always with the understanding that it will not be in *our* time.

The Clonigulane social took place on the last Friday before Lent at Ryan's Lounge down in the village. Four hundred tickets were sold in advance at three pounds each, and more people paid at the door. The parents and aunts and uncles and past pupils and friends of the school packed into the bar that night, coming to dance to pay off the roof. There were spot prizes, sponsored by the shopkeepers in the village, and drawings for bottles of wine, large umbrellas, boxes of chocolates, petrol vouchers, free hairdos, and a trailer of turf from Michael Downes. These were held between the set dances and the waltzes, while the plates of sandwiches each family had made moved through the crowds.

The school's debt for the roof was cleared that night. But the desks will have to wait for next year.

One morning, two weeks after the Clonigulane social, we were driving Deirdre down the road to school as usual. When we pulled over to collect Una, Colette, and Noel, the three Downes children, we heard the news. Pauline came out to tell us, her face distraught and pale: Master Cleary had died in his sleep during the night. Behind her as she spoke, the three young children stood staring at us with the terrible blankness of grief in children. They couldn't quite comprehend that the master was dead.

We returned home in shock. Death was not an infrequent event in an aging parish; throughout the winter especially there always seemed to be funerals streaming into one of the two funeral parlors at either end of the village. Only a month earlier, our friend Frank Saunders, a warm and kindly shopkeeper in his sixties, a very gentle man with welcome and sincerity always in his dealings, had died after a long battle with cancer, leaving a great sense of loss behind him in the village. A large proportion of the population was elderly, and from Christmas until Easter I sometimes imagined the outlying cottagers determinedly wintering out so many iron days of mist and rain, burning the turf and waiting for the brightness and the big lift of April's light.

News of the dead travels quickest here; the mass and funeral times follow the morning news on the local radio station. Chris and I, having come from outside, are not part of the intricate network that connects relations however distant and brings people in cars and on bicycles to funerals of those they might scarcely have met from one year to the next. It is a genuine thing, the grieving and the comforting. It is not uncommon for a busload of parishioners to go for the day to a funeral "up the country" somewhere if the deceased was a close relative of someone in the parish. And when he is someone well known, like Frank Saunders, and now Master Cleary, whose life had been lived in and for the parish, then everything stops. The whole landscape for miles around seems to pause and mourn.

The funeral mass for Kieran Cleary was held in the community center that was serving as the church while St. Michael's Church across the street was being renovated. The pews were ranged down the hall in front of the stage, and rows of seats had been set out in the back across the badminton court. The thirty-six children of Clonigulane School sat in the front rows with Mrs. Callinan. Each of them had been asked to bring a daffodil. A rosary was begun by a lone man's voice somewhere and immediately voices swelled into the prayers. Here and there throughout the crowd were some of the master's recent past pupils, several of them, boys and girls of thirteen and fourteen, with faces puffy from tears. At the head of the church sat Annette Cleary and her four daughters, the youngest eight years old. "God'll take care of you," whispered the woman next to me. "That's the last thing he told her."

Five priests said the mass. Father Linnane, our curate for many years, had come back from his new parish for the service, as had a cousin of the master's, a priest from England.

"As you know," said Father Malone, "Kieran was my right-hand man, and like Annette and the children and everyone else I'll miss him terribly. We had the Clonigulane social not long ago and of course it was a great success. After it was over and the debt had been cleared, Kieran turned to me and said, 'Well, Father, I can die a happy man now. The only thing left for me to save is my soul.'"

To any who had known him it was easy to hear and see Master Cleary in his shy, self-deprecating way, his head turned to one side and his voice low and a little unsure, his eyebrows lifting as if flicking upward the endless uncertainty of the world to see how the toss would land.

The five children whom he had prepared for confirmation this year brought up the gifts for the offertory—along with the bread and wine was a Gaelic football for lately he had often joined in the games in the yard. The master was a fair goalkeeper, Karol Downes had told me. A flute played in the choir, lonesome and melancholic. A cousin of the master's, a man with a drained-looking face and blue suit, struggled to read a poem, his voice breaking up as he moved off into the side room. Streams of tears flowed throughout the hall now. The mass ended. The children stood up with their daffodils and followed the coffin out into the main street of the village.

In two lines behind the master's coffin, the children of Clonigulane walked with their daffodils down the street to the graveyard behind Cleary's house, and behind them again the road filled with people passing the closed shops and the post office. No cars drove up or down. At the crossroads, up from Kieran's home, the funeral paused. The wind blew bitterly. The daffodils in the children's hands were bent over. Six more men shouldered the coffin and again we moved on, into the old graveyard. Silence and wind and the emptiness of the landscape, uncovered heads, downcast eyes. Within a moment the coffin was lowered in. A handful of the schoolchildren took out their tin whistles and played an air the master had taught them. People bit their lips, children began to cry. Father Malone ushered them forward to the graveside. "Don't be afraid," he said. "Come on, that's it." And so they came singly, and then in pairs, to throw their daffodils down into the grave.

It was over. Turning away, my hands on the shoulders of Deirdre and the Downes girls, I was remembering something I had read in the booklet celebrating the centenary of the Clonigulane School. There, Kieran Cleary had written about changes in education since 1951, when he became principal.

We were more severe than we meant to be, or intended to be. "But if severe in aught, the love we bore for learning was at fault." When corporal punishment was banned in schools it changed what was to many a house of torture into a school where kindness, encouragement, caring, respect for authority, and a desire for learning and a sense of humor took the place of the instrument of punishment, and as many of us found out, too late, but not too late for future generations, there is no child who is not eager to learn. We would all love a second "bite of the cherry" but nobody gets that. Most would live differently if given a second chance.

Walking away from the funeral that day, I thought of those words, their regret and self-doubt, and looking around at the faces of the young and old coming sadly out through the Kilmihil graveyard, thought: The master needn't have worried. Leaving the graveyard, I could not imagine a Clonigulane master half a century from now with a life given to the rural school.

We have visitors. For a couple of mornings now, two pheasants, a male and a female, have come into the front garden. There have been pheasants before, and quite often in the evening a bird might startle into the sky as we approach along the Kiltumper road. But these are different. They seem to be always there, crossing the lawn and stopping to look up at us looking down on them. When they come they give the morning a wonderful tranquillity. It is not only the beautiful plumage of the male or the pride of his walk, but something in their pairing that is fine, too, the way they accompany each other on their daily tour before heading back into the grove. I am thrilled that we have been so blessed as to have these visions in the garden each morning.

A few days ago I noticed a large blue plastic container in the field. It had been set up on small sticks, and falling from holes in its bottom was a scattering of oats.

"Someone's feeding them," I told Niall. "Someone brought them there and is feeding them."

"Must be the Gun Club," he said. "They're hoping they'll have chicks in the wild."

"Right there by our house? In the Grove?"

"Yes."

"Well, when the time comes, I'm not going to let them shoot them."

"It won't be until late autumn anyway."

"I'll bring them in. We'll hide them."

"Yes, let's hide them, Mammy," said Deirdre.

"In the autumn, Deirdre," I said, wondering what I was letting myself in for while gazing down at the two innocents browsing beautifully through the fuchsia. They held the promise and hope of spring for me—of life renewed—a life I was learning to cherish because of its simplicity and honesty. Easter was upon us and the symbols of resurrection were present everywhere. Even up in Clonigulane, there was a sense of hope as Mrs. Callinan and the board of management kept the school in good spirits while a replacement for the master was being talked about everywhere. Undoubtedly, the new teacher would be young, and new life would be breathed into the old school. I had great plans for repainting its two rooms and went about my day envisioning the children's cloakroom at Clonigulane in sky blue with round puffs of white clouds floating above their heads. Hope springs eternal.

It was Easter break for Deirdre, our birthdays were coming up, and we two were going to visit my family in the U.S. It would be a treat for my mother to see us, as she rarely gets to visit us here. The boys would stay behind. (Niall said something about throwing Joseph's bottle into the fire in a ceremonial male-bonding thing.)

Deirdre and I flew out from Shannon to New York on my birthday. My godmother, Eileen Brown, had remembered Deirdre's birthday, which is four days after mine, and sent her a wonderful children's book called *Emily* by Michael Bedard and Barbara Cooney, which is about the poet Emily Dickinson. We took it on the plane with us and after reading only a couple of pages Deirdre said that it sounded like poetry—and this before the child in the story discovers who the woman in the window is. Now whether my daughter is a genius at six, or the words and pictures succeed sublimely I'm not sure. But the real coincidence occurred just after this, when I spotted Eavan Boland sitting a few seats in front of us. Eavan is Ireland's premier woman poet, now finally getting some highly deserved recognition for her outstanding work. Unlike the Emily in the story, who is reticent, wispy, and ethereal, dressed in long white frocks, Eavan has a reputation for being outspoken and forthright. That day she was dressed comfortably in a dark jacket and skirt and black blouse. Her red hair had been quickly brushed. I remembered her as exactly the same from my student days in Dublin a long time ago, years before I even met Niall. I was intimidated by her then. Her ferocious energy inspired quite a few of us students in the School of Irish Studies. I was even more in awe of her now.

"You know, Deirdre," I whispered, "when you grow up and go to Daddy's school you will be reading and studying that woman's poetry." I can't remember who suggested it, me or Deirdre, but I agreed that I would introduce myself to her, talk with her if she remembered me, and ask her to sign Deirdre's book.

So I summoned the courage and introduced myself, reminding Eavan Boland of the days, nearly twenty years earlier, when we had shared afternoons together in Sandymount and Ballsbridge with David Green, Michael Coffey, Terry Rogers, Susan Ward, and Michael Quinlin (all of whom are presently writers in their own right) drinking coffee and Guinness, smoking cigarettes, and speaking of poetry. We talked for a while and when she left she signed Deirdre's book with best wishes.

✦ SIX ✦

Nancy and Nellie are in love. This is Deirdre's conclusion today, hearing the racket Nellie is making from inside the high fuchsias in the back meadow. Nancy, our young mare, is gone from her, taken in the back of a horsebox off to East Clare to an appointment with a twenty-year-old stallion named Pride of Tomes. Nellie, the donkey, left behind, roars inconsolably whenever one of us walks past outside, and to hear her braying, the sound so full of ache and heartbreak, it is not difficult to imagine that she is in love.

It wasn't always so. When Nancy, a three-quarter thoroughbred chestnut mare was first given to us by Chris's father, Joe, we still had cows on the farm. But Nancy was too fine a lady to mix with them. In those first days she flicked back her ears and high-trotted around the back paddock, startled by everything, it seemed. Then, once she had settled in, she stood for long periods at the gate, just gazing toward the back window of the cottage. Chris decided that she was lonely.

"What ye need, then, is a donkey, Crissie," Mary Breen told her.

And a few days later we found out from Martin Keane about an elderly neighbor of his, a Mr. O'Leary, who owned a donkey that we could have as company for Nancy. So, one spring afternoon, I went to Greygrove with a length of blue rope and met Nellie. She was cornered in the field, and I awkwardly slipped the rope over her head. Mr. O'Leary, a thin man, crinkled his weathered face in a smile as I caught her. He seemed delighted—whether because he knew something he wasn't telling about the donkey, or because he was genuinely pleased that she was going to a good home and would have the company of Nancy, I couldn't tell. He would take no money for her and simply waved Nellie and me away. She set off at a trot, and I, knowing nothing about leading asses, trotted along behind her. It was two miles back to Kiltumper. Nellie tugged and pulled with such strength that I soon realized there was no way I could hold her back, so we lit off along the road, Nellie trotting at full speed and I running at the end of the rope. By the time we reached the Kiltumper road I had picked up some of the Downes children, who delightedly shrieked and galloped alongside me as I tried to slow the donkey down. But she was having none of it. Nellie was freed, she thought, or close to it, and was going full steam ahead.

With Noel Downes now pulling on the rope with me, and Una and Colette trailing behind, Nellie and I arrived at the gateway to our farm, where Chris and Deirdre stood waiting to let the new arrival in to lonely Nancy. Nellie reached the gate and Nancy saw her—and with a single turn reared, leapt the five-bar gate out of the paddock, and raced into the Big Meadow! She fled, terrified—or insulted—by this new companion. Nellie began roaring and Nancy ran off, high-stepping, nostrils flaring, until she was at the far corner of the five-acre meadow.

It seemed a complete mismatch. For although the shaggy gray donkey was perhaps smitten, the fine mare would not stay in the same field with her.

And so began the slow and gradual courtship of their made match. Nellie was hidden in a shed. Nancy was put in the stable, and only when she was securely tied was Nellie brought out on a rope and fastened where Nancy could see her. It took days until, tentatively, they would each eat from the same hay bale, from opposite sides. There was still some snorting and flaring, but a truce seemed to have been established. After four days we let the two of them out into the paddock. Nancy raced off and Nellie trotted behind. A month later, I noticed that whenever we moved Nancy, if Nellie was not with her, the mare became restless and anxious, trotting along the hedges looking for the donkey. They needed each other, and it was soon impossible to bring Nancy down to her stable without bringing Nellie alongside too and parking her somewhere under the sycamore trees where

Nancy could look out and see her. As unlikely a pair as you could imagine!

Nellie's braying today tears through the spring afternoon, and Deirdre runs up to her swing with her hands over her ears as Joseph makes little leaps to the sound and utters mini-brays himself. I tell Nellie across the gate that Nancy will be back, but wonder: What will happen if a foal is born?

We are waiting to see who will be the new principal in Clonigulane. Among the rumors that have run around the townland, one is that some of the parents are insisting it be a man: a master. Like all rumors it is nearly impossible to pin down.

When I told it to Chris she was shocked.

"But you can't say that nowadays. You can't say the principal has to be a man. What's wrong with its being a woman anyway?"

"I suppose," I said, defending the indefensible, "they feel two women in the school without a man would be . . ." My voice trailed off, as I was unable quite to figure out what the conclusion should be.

"Well, we should tell Father Malone."

"What?"

"In case he thinks that's what all the parents in the school want. We should tell him."

The following morning, I met Father Malone coming out of the church after ten o'clock mass. Hands in his jacket pockets as always, he stood in front of me outside the old post office, and in the first moment of my approach a brief flicker of apprehension crossed his face. Even as the feeling arose he quashed it, like a person who had diligently trained himself to overcome acute shyness.

"Morning, Niall."

"Father."

"The play went well."

"It did, Father, very well."

"Lot of people talking about it, some hoping to see it again."

"That's the way to leave them, Father."

"That's right, Niall."

The two of us stood there, the wind flicking a wisp of his thin hair, his hand brushing it down.

"Father?"

"Yes?"

"Father, I wanted . . . well, Chris and I wanted . . . to just let you know, there's a rumor that the parents all want a man . . ."

Pause. No sign of acknowledgment or denial or surprise on Father Malone's face.

". . . Well, for our part, it doesn't matter, and whoever is best qualified, man or woman, is all that counts."

He looked away for a moment, the lock of hair blowing free again and crossing his brow. He blinked and then nodded. "Well, thank you, Niall. You understand I can't make any comment on that now one way or the other."

"Oh certainly, Father."

"I can't you see."

"No no, not at all."

A large, square woman came down the street along the path. We both saluted her. Then Father Malone nodded again.

"One way or the other. I can't."

"No, no, and I don't want you to, Father. I just wanted to let you know."

"I understand, Niall, but I can't make any comment. There'll be interviews before a board and that . . ."

"Yes, Father, that's grand."

"So I'll have to leave it to that."

"Right so, Father."

"Right so. Goodbye, Niall."

When I returned to Chris I replayed the meeting line by line.

"Well," she said when I had finished, "what do you think that means?"

"It means," I said, "we'll have to wait and see. I'm sure some of the parents want a master because there was always a master. But there aren't that many men primary school teachers anymore."

"Unless . . . there's Martin Keane," said Chris.

Martin is a bachelor in his thirties, a past pupil at Clonigulane School, who has been teaching for years in Ennis. He was now finishing a master's in education at Trinity in Dublin. He lives in the next townland, Greygrove. Chris wanted to persuade him to apply for the principal's position.

"Maybe," I said dubiously.

"Well," said Chris, "I'm going to talk to him. He'd be a wonderful *master.*

The key in the back door turns, there is no knock, the door opens. We know already who it is.

"I've a bag of burds at the back door for ye, missus," Martin Keane mimics in his best West Clare farm accent as he breezes into the kitchen, hopping down our two concrete and flag steps in his knee-high farm Wellingtons.

"Two guinea fowl, one bantam, and a cockerel!" He grins and throws his heavy bunch of keys onto the pine table, as he always does, and sits down on the couch on the far side of the fire.

Martin's entrance never varies. He makes his journey from door to couch in one confident, uninterrupted movement, keys dangling in midair, landing thump in the same place. He is one of the few friends we have who continues to make a *cuaird*, an unannounced visit, to our house. Usually he comes on Sunday evenings.

We enjoy his visits immensely as we share many interests. He is knowledgeable and well-read, and manages a full-time teaching job in Ennis and a full-time farm with incredible finesse. In this busy schedule Martin also sets aside time for his eleven-plus greyhounds, which he both breeds and races, and for coaching the badminton club, and for looks-in at our group's drama productions. He is Woody Allenesque in appearance—but with shorter hair—and very wry. Martin could be accused of being a cynic, a quality that distinguishes him from many people here because he isn't a *closet* skeptic or moaner. One thing one can always count on about Martin is that he will speak his mind. That I tend to do the same means that our conversations together always go directly to the point. It is Martin who sometimes refers to me as "Bullshit Breen"— meaning I don't employ any.

In every other household around the townland there are parents wondering if Martin will apply for the vacant post at Clonigulane. But few of them, I think, will ask him directly—it's the Irish habit of avoiding any embarrassing awkwardness at all costs.

Niall goes outside to put our new collection of fowl into the cabin. "So, Martin," I say, even before he has taken his first chocolate chip cookie (I baked them this afternoon, guessing he might arrive), "are you going to apply for the job or not?"

Martin can't help a broad grin at my directness.

"What job is that, missus?"

"Very funny, Martin. No, come on."

He looks pointedly at me, then says simply, ""No." He picks up the cookie and crunches it.

"How come?"

At this point Niall, who has returned, joins in with, "Perhaps, Martin, you'd like another cookie?"

"Thank you, Mr. Williams."

"Martin?"

"Yes, Chris?" Martin sighs and looks at me again. "It's like this," he continues, getting serious. "I don't know."

"I know what you're thinking. It's your decision and I'm not going to urge you to take it, but I just want to let you know that I think you'd be great, and if you do apply for it . . ."

"If you apply for it, you'll get it," Niall interrupts, "and when you do we'd like to be involved, all right?"

"All right."

I realize, as Martin certainly does, that it will be a major commitment for him to narrow his life's focus to the two-room schoolhouse down the road from his house. He is still single and will be giving up the freedom of the wider community of Ennis. He already has a secure teaching job. But I believe strongly in his ability to bring us a contemporary outlook as well as to bring his many talents to fulfillment at our rural hundred-year-old school.

"Martin," I can't stop myself from repeating, several cookies later, "you'd be TERRIFIC!"

One Saturday afternoon in early May, the townland waited to hear the results of the interviews for the master's vacant place. I brought Deirdre over to play at the Millars'. They are a young family living a couple miles from us, who, while not blow-ins like us, are not farmers either. Sean Millar is an air traffic controller at Shannon, and Ann is an avid gardener and an expectant mother. Vanessa, their first child, is Deirdre's best friend. Ann had attended Clonigulane as a child and was keenly interested in the appointment of a new principal. "Martin's at three o'clock," she said.

On the way back I stopped in at Mary Breen's. She was out

in the garden as usual, her white head appearing among the pinks of her flowers and a clutch of weeds in her hand. "Are you coming in, Niall?"

"I won't stop the work, Mary."

"No news of Martin yet, I suppose?"

"When was he due to go in? Three o'clock?"

"That's right, Niall. I suppose we won't know until tonight sometime."

"I'm sure he'll get it."

"You wouldn't know, Niall, you couldn't be sure. There's a few good ones going for it."

"There are. But I think Martin has the strongest chance."

The other candidates were all national school teachers with connections to the parish. They were either teaching in one of the three other schools in Kilmihil, or had found work in schools further up the country, waiting for an opportunity like this one to return as principal.

In the village everything was quiet that afternoon. At the end of the street, just up from the crossroads, two members of the Department of Education were sitting with Father Malone in his parlor interviewing the short-listed candidates. There was an inbreath taken in the townlands out the road around the school. The appointment of the principal would have a significant effect on the ongoing life of the school, its character, and atmosphere.

When Martin finally decided to apply for the job, we were very pleased, as were our neighbors. It was not that the other candidates were any the less deserving. It was for some simply the case that he was local and a man. For others it was because he was related to them. And for the rest of us, hope was born of his youth and energy, his openness to new ideas, and the breath of fresh air he would bring to the old school.

So that Saturday afternoon while he went down to Father Malone's house for his interview we waited. And later in the evening when the word came from Pauline Downes that Martin had been appointed principal of Clonigulane National School, we couldn't help but celebrate, feeling hope and expectation. And, of course, Martin's decision, his commitment, seemed a validation of our own.

In an effort to help make things more vibrant in the village I offered to design and plant a small garden plot on either side of the renovated church. My offer was taken up immediately by Father Malone and the Tidy Towns Committee. As gardening is the thing I love to do most, I pored over the pages of many gardening books and magazines, looking for ideas and suitable plants. I suppose, like many novice garden designers of intermediate skill, my vision was larger than life. The resulting drawing was ambitious for a small village but not beyond us, I thought, and could have been fully realized if I had had easy access to a very good garden center. But the majority of people here require only red geraniums and summer bedding plants and the occasional perennial flowering shrub, so structural, specimen, and evergreen shrubs are not available. What I had envisioned for the church was a garden that would come to life during the six months of autumn and winter. And for that I needed evergreen shrubs, not the brief, showy flowering brooms and weigelas and spireas that look like a bunch of twigs for most of the year. It was foolish of me not to realize that if only a third of what was initially planned materialized then we were doing well, very well. "These things take time," said Father Malone.

When the plants that were ordered finally did appear, only a few of those on my list were included. And some of them looked only marginally alive. The poor *Malus floribundi* had withered leaves, and the *acer platinode globesum* had only two measly branches.

"Plant them anyway," said Larry and Niall. "You never know. Perhaps their vicinity to the church will help them to survive." I was doubtful.

The Cotters planted the tiny box hedge plants as soon as they arrived, and while to many eyes they seemed dwarfed in comparison to the church, I have faith that our hedge will eventually grow and fill out. Its triangular shape mirrors the formality of the new church wall on one side, the old wall on another side, and the church itself on the third side.

Our new friend, Jim Channon, a keen gardener like me and a tireless worker as well, helped me with all the planting. We hoped to have it finished before the official reopening of the church. So one day we went down in our rain slickers and Wellies with borrowed wheelbarrow and sand and peat and tree stakes and ties and bonemeal and gravel and plastic and bark mulch, and went to work planting about thirty small plants.

We also had the help of Michael Downes, who was working part-time for the winter on grounds maintenance at the vocational school. Larry had asked Michael to lend us a hand. It was ironic for both Jim and me that here was Michael, our friend and neighbor, who had often come to each of us at different times when we were starting out, having trouble with this cow or that field or whatnot, now helping us again, only this time under *our* guidance. Michael kept his cap turned sideways and chuckled under his breath as he wheeled the barrow back and forth and threw bonemeal and sand under the newly planted hedge. Here was something foreign to his own experience, for what need had he of gardens and expensive hedges and bark mulch, with the real work of farming ahead of him when he got home? He appreciated what we were doing but in a way it is true that Jim and I are just amateurs. Gardening is not our work. It is our hobby. And Michael is too busy for hobbies.

So into the box hedge we planted a weeping birch and a weeping pear, *Pyrus salisafolia pendula*, and a purple prunus instead of the autumn flowering cherry I would have liked. In my imagination I see these trees in the gravelled triangle underplanted with spring bulbs and euphorbias and helianthenum and hellebores. And in the shrubbery on the right-hand side of the church we planted a pink potentillas and a small hebe. Father Malone had announced from the altar that the church garden was in need of plants and anyone wishing to assist in any way was encouraged to make a floral donation. Mrs. Mangan had left her potentillas at the church door, and Lily Hourigan had brought her hebe up to Jim and me complete with a bag of bonemeal and a liter bottle of water. I think she was prepared to plant it herself and was much relieved to see us already at work.

We carried on with our planting and vowed that one day we would get the daphnes and the *Garrya elliptica* and the *Iris foetidisimia,* that the maintenance of the church garden would be an ongoing commitment, and that in time a committee of gardeners, novice and accomplished, would tend the garden. And it will be one that we will all be proud of.

For the past couple of years we have not cut or saved turf in Kiltumper. Instead, from Michael Downes' bog up the hill, we have bought trailerloads of machine-made turf and seen the backbreaking season of the bog pass us by. The machines—great caterpillar-wheel things with an extended arm or hopper trailers squeezing out long trails of black turf behind them like snakes—do the work in half an hour it took a man three days to do. On the bog next to ours, P.J. Coughlan's turf machines go from morning until night, spreading the hill fields and every other available place with gleaming brown ribbons of machine-turf. They blacken the fields and cover the grass in the late spring, cutting and spreading enough turf for forty or fifty families. The bog, meanwhile, is left in a devastated state, full of vast craters of black water where the machines have dug. But the machine-turf is good turf. For rather than the *sleans*man cutting the turf away in layers or bars as he descends to the quality fuel deep down, the machine makes a blend of the good and bad and presses out a uniform narrow sod that dries well and burns slow. This "sausage" turf, as it quickly became known, has almost completely taken over in the last ten years. The days when you hired a turfcutter with his *slean* have all but disappeared, and the likes of men like Michael Dooley and Michael Donnellan with their superb skill at cutting a bank are vanishing. This, too, is part of the change in the west. In Clare in another ten years the number of bogs where you can see a handcut turfbank will be few indeed.

Some years ago I would have lamented this change. The way of the turfcutter, his skill and place in the farming landscape, had always seemed so integral a part of the western lifestyle in places such as Kiltumper. His disappearance is like the disappearance of hedgerows or cattle—almost unthinkable. And yet three days' hard work cutting the family's fuel for the winter now can be done in thirty minutes! So, while the winged spades or turf *sleans* are left rusting in farm cabins and sheds, the turf talk turns to hoppers and sausage turf and big bogs of many acres replacing the old small family plots.

The truth is that machines make the life of the people easier. There are no boys in the classroom now who will make their summer wages with a *slean* and go on year after year to become that figure on the bog slowly, steadily turning out the sods onto the bank. Instead they all talk of tractors and machines, many of them already knowing more than their fathers. Change comes so quickly now where it had once been so slow.

It has been the same with the hay meadows. When we first arrived in Kiltumper, the number of families in the townland who saved hay the old traditional way, making high trams or cocks with two-pronged hayforks, hoping for fine weather in which to complete the task, was great indeed. We did not know then that we were on the very brink of change. As the weather that summer of 1985 worsened, rather than leave to waste the sopping hay, the farmers made long wedge slabs of silage and covered them with black plastic. We made one ourselves that summer under the falling skies of July. Within two years the majority of winter feed in Kiltumper was saved this way and farmers put down concrete slabs in their farm-yards for the silage. It was their way of beating the weather, for unlike hay, silage can be made in the rain that so often comes slowly misting in and settling over midsummer. The times when you can see men and women with hayforks in a meadow are few now, and growing rarer.

This year there has come a new change: In talking on the side of the road to Tom Hayes about saving the Big Meadow at the back of our house he said, without hesitation or worry about the weather, "I'll wrap it." To "wrap" the meadow— this is a new phrase for the latest farm technology to reach us. Wrapping machines bale the silage in manageable black plastic balls right in the meadows now. Where once a meadow lay stippled with golden hay trams there are now black plastic bales. And while it is impossible not to lament the change, the loss of the golden beauty of the hay meadows, of the moments sitting back against a tram with forks stuck in the ground looking back with neighbors across a meadow "saved," the whole feel and smell and air of hay, the scent and sensation, the whole meaning of summer in the stuff, I know the farmer's life is easier now. And the quality of the fodder better! The change is simply the natural progression of things.

Not a few of the older farmers claim that the weather itself has forced the change, that the climate has become ever more unpredictable, and that while ten or twenty years ago a farmer was more or less assured of a week or two of settled weather in July or August to save hay, this is no longer the case. This is not simply nostalgic reminiscence. Now rain truly comes more frequently, it seems, in July than in January. Simply to survive, change has been forced on the small farmer. Besides, I am told, it is unreal and romantic to want things to stay the same. Now Ireland is measuring itself against the other countries in the European Community. Do the Dutch or German farmers care to save their meadows with hayforks because it is more picturesque or traditional? No.

Yet isn't it just that, the old and traditional, the *un-mechanized* version of Ireland that so many of the German tourists who call at our house want to see? The needs of the farmer are one thing and those of the tourist industry something else. For the farmer facing the reality of a life in the west, the uncertainties of Irish weather mean baled silage will always be a better bet than saving hay, just as machine turf will always have an advantage over turf cut the old way with the *slean*. And yet, it seems there ought to be a way of conserving the older, more traditional lifestyle of the Irish farmer. It is even in the government's interest that turf and hay always be saved *somewhere*.

In another ten years, when Joseph is old enough to go to the bog on the hill of Upper Tumper, will there be a working *slean*sman left? Can I learn the skill in time? This year, aware that an ancient art is about to vanish, and feeling guilty for acceding to this change, as well as needing to find the cheapest way possible of getting our fuel, I asked Michael Donnellan for a day's cutting. A bachelor in his fifties with tufts of white hair above his ears and dazzling blue eyes, he agreed to come but told me the bogs were wet at the moment. Give it a week, he said. During that next week I suffered severe pains in my stomach and, afraid that I had a hernia, I did not get to the bog, nor did I see Michael again.

The weather was bright and windy when I was able to get down the road a way to pay a visit. In Mary Breen's kitchen I sat for cups of strong tea and chat.

"I told Michael I'd be on the bog with him, Mary, but I'm afraid I don't feel up to it at the moment."

"I told him about you, Niall; he said not to worry. We'll figure something out."

My part of the work on the bog would be to stand on the upper side of the bank and take away the sods as Michael cut them and threw them off the *slean* at my feet. I would fork them onto Michael's green wooden turf barrow and run away off across the bank to topple out the thirty or so sods of wet turf and get back in time to take away the ones he had cut in the meantime. In this way I was supposed to "keep it out" from him. It was donkey work, as hard in its way perhaps as the rhythmical press and cut and lift of his *slean* as Michael cut away the bars of the turf. I had done it before. A few years earlier he had cut turf for us and I had spent a few exhausting days pattering back and forth with the barrow. I knew what it was like—how he worked without pause, lowering himself down towards the watery bar peak where the best turf lay beneath the surface; how he slipped off his boots and changed to Wellingtons, the small woolen hat shielding his head from sun and wind; the break when we heard the call of the cuckoo.

It was another ten days before I felt well enough to take a

walk up through the hill fields in the evening and out across the Christmas tree meadow to the bog. When I arrived on the hilltop I could already see his turf for the year was cut, the edge of his bank like a long cut of chocolate cake, impossibly straight and sheer, forty yards long and six feet down. Michael's skill with the *slean* was such that the whole thing, the thousand small spadings of the *slean*, were like one neat incision, as if a giant knife had taken out a piece of the bogland in one go. You might have said it was the work of a machine, so clean and perfect was the edge of the bank, until you walked further and looked across the boundary wire at the great scooped watery holes in the bog that Coughlan's machines left behind them.

They were still working on into the evening with the hoppers, spreading the turf as I walked over to our own bank. I was surprised. Michael had cut the top bars of our turf and now they were stacked along the bank, four sods high. He had laid them one on top of the other for me, doing all he could alone. I took off my sweater and brought out the barrow from the cluster of heather where Michael had parked it. Using my bare hands to gather the wet and slippery-soft sods of the turf, I plopped them one after the other onto the barrow and spread them for drying. I worked for two hours at my own pace and was greatly relieved not to be rushing back and forth to keep pace with the *slean*sman. But still, in the movement of each slow sod from the edge of the bank to the heathery places where I hoped it would dry, was the presence of Michael Donnellan.

The following day I told Mary how delighted I had been to find the turf cut. "Now, Niall," she said with a smile. With less surprise but with immense gratitude and appreciation I

went up to the bog a week later and found the same thing—
that Michael had been there before me, coming from his
house up on the hill through Melicans' forestry and over the
wire fence to cut another bar of my turf and lay it out there to
await me. He knew I hadn't been well, though he and I had
never spoken of it. He knew the barrow work might have
been impossible for me this year, and so he cut the turf for
Chris and me, appearing and disappearing like a pixie. And I
walked down the hill fields of Tumper with turf-blackened
hands to the fading thrumming of the sausage machines.

Deirdre has been preparing for weeks now for her first ballet
exam. She came out from class one day so excited. A man
was coming over from London to watch them so they had to
be at school two hours ahead of time because they were
going to "do their hair and put on makeup and everything."

A man coming over from London? What could that mean?
She must not have that right, I thought. Then I discovered
that she *was* right, that a representative from London's
Royal Academy of Dance was flying in to oversee the examinations. Only those pupils Ms. Dinan thought would pass
the exam were asked to participate. When the parents were
invited to see the preprimary class practice a week before
the big day, I was thrilled. And impressed at how able they
were. How confident the tiny troupe was, running and stop-

ping in time to the music in all the right places, pointing and tapping toes, twirling on tiptoes and curtsying—all without the slightest sound or signal from Ms. Dinan. They had learned their movements by heart but what impressed me the most was their grasp of the meter of the music.

On the day of the exam, Deirdre arrived at the school two hours early. I had to leave her there, with her ironed socks and skirt and leotard and scrubbed-cleaned slippers and her hairnet and hairpins. When I returned in three hours, she and the others were just coming out. The nod from Ms. Dinan to the mothers waiting told us they had all done well. And the beautiful, proud face of Deirdre as she appeared through the doorway with her hair in a braided bun on top of her head with two little blue bows and the number eight pinned to her leotard is a lasting memory for me. Two weeks later we heard that she had passed and that she received a special mention: "Beautiful run and pause, Deirdre."

+ SEVEN +

On a Saturday evening in May, having made a trip up to Dublin, I went with my father to mass in the Kilmacud church down the road where I had gone every week when I was growing up. It is a suburban church, a large, high red-bricked building in an upper-middle-class parish. I can remember its being built. I remember being in the small stone church that is next to it, now turned into a combination scout's hall and greengrocer. I think I remember Latin masses. I remember the crush of people in that small building, the stained-glass windows, the heat of bodies, a young and expanding parish in the late sixties. When the new church was being built, so huge were the excavations that the old church next to them was dwarfed. We went over and played inside the unfinished walls; we walked inside the massive hall, our imaginations making it a great indoor football field, a place in which you could get to top speed running full tilt from the slightly raised platform that was to be the altar down to and out the new plastic-wrapped doors that flapped after you when they closed.

When the church itself "moved in," it took on another life, as the old and more decorative place behind it looked sadly deserted, suddenly absent of God. As a child I felt the older place was forlorn. How was it that the church where I had prayed so fervently, with screwed-up eyes, scrubbed face, and clean quiff to my hair had turned into this? It was a first lesson of a kind: that God didn't make his own house and could be moved.

It was a time of prosperity and growth. Dublin was swelling, and housing estates were moving in red blocks ever further out the country roads toward the mountains. On Sunday drives my father would be like some astonished mapmaker, taking the car along roads that were changing almost before our eyes as he pointed out to my mother the new developments. Nothing, it seemed, was changing as quickly as Dublin, and still, despite this growth and change, the certainty of religion and religious practice seemed firm. When my parents took us to ten or eleven o'clock mass in the new Kilmacud church—no Saturday evening masses then—the place was packed. Microphones and speakers had to be employed to bring the priest's voice to the men standing outside the side doors.

I remembered the church as part of my growing up and

adolescence. Although I had never quite forgiven the church building itself for replacing the old stone one, I had taken my thoughts there at several key times in a most natural and free way, kneeling under the high vaulted roof to ask for good examination results or a football win, or when my grandfather was ill, to pray. It was part of me, as I suppose churches were of all those children who grew up in my generation.

And so, that evening, going with my father back down to Kilmacud church for mass, I felt more forcibly than I can say a deep sadness on seeing the church more than three-quarters empty. I sat there and kept waiting for the crowd to come in. In a church that could seat well over a thousand there were less than two hundred. As the mass began and the congregation made the responses, their voices were muffled. There were no teenagers in the pews. Coming from the older people who made up the congregation, the prayers seemed to take on the quality of melancholy.

I was reminded of all of this again when I returned to Kilmihil. Here, too, this year we'd had a moving church. And in a few days it was going to move back into the renovated building.

The Duggans were painting their shop in preparation. Helena was wondering about green doors for the butcher's. The Kirks were painting and so were the Fitzpatricks and Cussens. If you stood in the middle of the street and looked up and down you felt the whole village was a hive of activity. At the two traffic islands that stand at the western end of the village, Chris was planting purple beech trees. Flower baskets were set hanging and window boxes potted up. Kilmihil was transforming itself between rain showers on the few dry days that came at the end of May. I had never seen the village looking better. Was it the influence of the Tidy Towns season? It was not. It was the bishop coming.

For the occasion of the reopening of the parish church of St. Michael's, Bishop Harty was to arrive in Kilmihil on the last Friday in May for the rededication ceremony. It was an event in parish history. There had been a church on the site since 1831, when a Father Timothy Kelly had written himself into local history by announcing to his parishioners that construction would start on a church in the village and there would be collections toward its cost beginning the following Sunday. Local stories have it that the announcement was met with considerable doubt, but that Father Timothy arrived on the scene in the morning while the local volunteer builders were standing around and threw himself into the work. A beggar, watching, is said to have then come forward and given whatever money he had, saying, "God bless the work." And from then on, there was never a difficulty until the church was completed.

St. Michael's had been closed throughout the winter with the builders in occupation. The church edifice had been in serious disrepair. The timber galleries at the two sides, above the ladies' aisle and the men's, were rotten and needed to be replaced; the roof beams were dangerous as well. And so the parishioners had moved out and the builders moved their machinery and sand and cement inside the high wall of the church grounds in the center of the village.

Stories leaked out as to how the construction was going. "The roof is completely rotten," I was told one morning by a man outside the post office. "The floor is being thrown out," said another. "Those old Victorian quarry tiles—red, black, and ochre—sure they're all cracked and ruined." "The more they do, the more they'll find wrong, Niall," said a woman at Mrs. Fitzgerald's, looking out the window across at the heap of rubble and wondering sadly when she'd see the inside of her church again. For the fact was that no sooner was it announced that the church needed renovation than it seemed everyone had an opinion on what should or shouldn't be done. But by and large disputes were confined to kitchen conversations and rarely, if ever, brought up before Father Malone. It was he, after all, who had announced from the altar the necessity of carrying out the work, and he, as head of the parish council, who was responsible for seeing it completed.

I was reminded, of course, of the old Kilmacud church when the congregation moved from it, and wondered if there were boys and girls in the village who passed the old church feeling God was still in there amidst the scaffolding and not across the street in the hall.

As it turned out, mass in the community center hall was in a way more precious for being more fragile; it was less imposing somehow and had a kind of shared intimacy through the winter and early spring. But the parishioners never forgot their church, and the date of its reopening was a constant topic. It would reopen for St. Patrick's Day. Then they were hoping to have it ready for Easter. And then May 24th.

There was in this case a more tangible cause for concern than mere faith or the love of the parishioners for their church. The renovations cost approximately £180,000. The weekly collections in this parish generally amounted to something close to £300. Kilmihil is a relatively poor parish. There were no wealthy sponsors to help defray the costs. So

Father Malone had sent a pack of twelve monthly envelopes to each house in the parish. A second set of envelopes followed the first. And while there were the usual half-complaints and cross-talk about the price of it, and what did we really know about what was going on inside the church walls, there with the builders, still the envelopes came in.

St. Michael's Church before the renovations had been old-fashioned and full of warm feeling. Up the long aisle there had been wainscotting and an archway of exposed beams. Behind the altar had been painted a combination of yellow and two shades of pink and gold that had struck Chris as most unusual and beautiful when we first stepped inside the door. Now, it had all been redone; what would have changed?

The evening of the proper and official return to the church marked a special moment in the village's life. Every-thing was set. Only the night before, while Chris was practicing in the choir upstairs, Paddy Cotter had been moving his ladder and hammering up the new stations of the cross. The interior was sparkling white now with peach accents. It was fresh and clean.

Bishop Harty led nine other priests and Father Malone up the long aisle and the choir sang to the packed church. You could feel a swell of pride among many parishioners. The village, in all its freshly painted newness, hushed to the hymns. There was a note of reaffirmation and hope, a stay against decline and loss, the putting down of a mark that in its own way was as momentous and historic as the first stones Father Timothy had picked off the heap. The renovations assured the church's future, and while I had been so forcibly struck when in Dublin at the near emptiness of the vast red-brick church in the parish where I grew up, there was no sense in Kilmihil this May evening of a weakening of faith.

"There is a lot of shallow thinking in Ireland," said Bishop Harty from the altar, "even in high places, and a pathetic tendency to copy thinking and policies that have failed in other countries. There is a lack of feeling often for the power of genuine religion to enhance human nature and human sensibility. The prevailing attitude seems to be that if you can't express everything in the coinage of the marketplace, then you should ignore it. But the best antidote to shallow thinking at national level is honest thinking at local level and a strong sense of place. Unless we have this sense of place, we are not likely to make any significant service to our country, Europe, or the world. A sense of place gives us a certain stability and above all a means of measuring the new ideas set before us. We are not likely to surrender to fads and fashions if we are firmly rooted in a community with a proper sense of its past. Only in the close interaction of home, school, and parish can we teach the lasting lessons that will banish the violence, greed, and permissiveness that threaten the survival of Irish society."

The congregation listened without a murmur.

"The renovation of this church could not have been undertaken if you did not have a strong sense of place, a sense of belonging to a particular community and people. You have kept faith with the past in making your own sacrifices in carrying out this thorough renovation. You have respected the clean strong lines of the original church but transformed it into a warm, welcoming, bright church with a more intimate relationship between sanctuary and congregation. Let it be a much-used church, opening out onto the street of your town, let it be an invitation to stop and pray a while, and may the young and old accept that invitation frequently."

Silence fell. Then the choir sang and all the lights in the church of St. Michael the Archangel were lit. Afterwards Bishop Harty joined the neighboring priests and the parishioners in a stroll through the village and across into the community center to meet the people and have tea and cakes. The mood grew into one of celebration and achievement, and nobody who came or went by Church Street past the newly painted shops and houses and the new trees and the flowering shrubs could help but feel it.

✦ EIGHT ✦

SAVE CRANNY POST OFFICE: SAVE A RURAL COMMUNITY, YOURS COULD BE NEXT. The sign on the road to Ennis had been put up in reaction to the rumor that *An Post*, our postal service, was planning to save money by cutting back on the rural subpost offices, opening them only three days a week. Such post offices did very little business outside dole or pension day and were cost-ineffective to keep open all week, they said.

This struck at the heart of many debates on the West. The post office had a social function as well as an economic one. The rural post offices in small villages were like central intelligence; whatever had happened or was happening about the parish was usually known in the post office first and from there the news went out. This was partly a remnant of the days not long ago when the telephone exchange was also run by the local postmaster. If the "business" of the morning in many small villages was totalled at only a few stamps and a few newspapers, the value of the chat and news greatly outweighed it.

Should such places then be subsidized and kept open although they are not operating "cost-effectively"? What would happen to these communities if the subpost offices closed? The government didn't have an answer for that.

Chris and I arrived in Kiltumper on the point of this change. When we first moved into the cottage our telephone was operated by a crank handle on the side that we twirled to get Connie or old Tom Fitzgerald, Gregory's late father, down in the village post office. Despite the inherent difficulties of the system there were unexpected benefits. Occasionally we might ask to be put through to the Blakes only to be told that their car had passed by the post office and they'd probably gone over to the Saunderses' and the call would be put through there instead. Telephone exchanges have since been automated throughout the country.

Likewise, when we first arrived, P. J. Crowley, the postman, walked up from his van to every house he had letters for, and carried with him the news along the road. For many of the elderly farmers and their wives in the more remote corners of the parish he might be the only other face of the day. Now green plastic letter boxes are being distributed by *An Post* to be put at the ends of avenues or driveways in the same way they are in America, and P. J.'s van slips away along the road without a stop for conversation.

All these changes, while necessary on some economic level, no doubt, are weakening the relationships that hold communities together here. The very fabric of rural life is becoming threadbare, Chris says. The Cranny sign on the Ennis road expresses this concern, but I sensed a glimmer of hope and resolve among the local people who were going to fight for their post office. On the following Sunday, in the Kilmihil Parish newsletter given out at mass, there was a notice that read: IT'S YOUR POST OFFICE: USE IT OR LOSE IT.

The fight goes on.

Rain again. So what else is new? Twenty-seven hours of sunshine were recorded for July! But boy, do the good days stand out like shiny gum wrappers on the long wet road. There was an evening recently that I will never forget. The full moon was rising over the Grove between the sycamore and ash. There was just enough light, and the white and pink flowers of the garden looked neon among the dark greeny shapes that circled the lawn. The air was cool and warm at the same time. The sky was midnight blue. I stood in the garden and soaked in it. A cuckoo was singing.

"Evening, Mr. Williams."

"Mr. Cassidy."

"Have you made your move?"

"I have."

"Right so, let me see here now."

I took the miniature chessboard down from the dresser shelf and laid it before him on the table. While he was looking at it I went to get the change for the bread. Deirdre and Joseph were chasing between the two rooms. The engine of the bread van outside was running.

To date we had played fifteen games and the score was fifteen to none. Nothing I could invent by way of a chess attack seemed capable of taking John Cassidy by surprise. He was always two or more moves ahead of me, and although I had two days to his two minutes to look at the board, I still seemed to be attacking like some leaden slow-motion boxer up against the real thing while he moved quickly and surely, at times even warning me if my move was going to lead me into difficulties three or four moves later. My chance lay in trying to play on his perception of my weakness as an opponent; if I could divert him with a flawed move perhaps he would miss for a moment the possibility that had opened up for me.

All afternoon I had been waiting for this moment, coming back in from the garden to check on the position and making sure that I was right. Yes, if I played my rook into this vulnerable position and he supposed it was a simple error, then in one surprise move I could mate him.

He stood over the table looking down. The bread van was waiting. I had told Chris earlier in the day that there was a chance for me in the game tonight and so she, too, was waiting on the steps of the kitchen.

"I see," said John. "Well, sorry about this, Mr. Williams, but I'll have to take that." He took the rook, and turned to go. "See you now."

"Wait a minute, Mr. Cassidy. I know my next move."

"You do?"

I pushed forward the queen.

"Checkmate."

"What?" He leaned on the table with his two fists and stared at the board for a second. Then he turned abruptly and offered me his hand. "Well done," he said, his face red.

"I wouldn't have beaten you if . . ."

"No no, fair play . . . I didn't even see it," he said, shaking his head and going out the door in a fluster.

The moment he had gone I leapt into the air. Deirdre and Joseph came from the parlor to see what was happening and did little leaps and jumps, too. It was a drizzling summer evening, the score was fifteen to one, and the bread van gone down the road would be back to start a new game on Friday.

While it is true that machines have made the cutting of turf easier no one has yet come up with an easier way to turn it and stack it. As Chris says, "It is *hand*made, one hundred percent Irish."

This is slow, laborious work as each sod must first be spread or turned on the bank, and only when the weather has caused a crust to form on it can it then be "footed" or stood on end against a few others to dry. This year the wet summer has made the drying slower. In the village the talk is of the rain and how wet the bogs have become, soaking up the ruined season like a great sponge of melancholy. In the waiting weeks, while any hope of making hay is abandoned to the silage wrappers, the turf talk goes on.

The season begins in May when the turf is cut but really goes into full swing in July when the national schools get their holidays and the children are freed into the promise of the long days and short nights of summer. The turf that has been cut a month or two earlier is normally ready for footing, and on dry mornings whole families pack into cars, bring lunch, and head for the bog.

Down the road, Michael and Pauline Downes and their five children go to the bog every dry day as they try to save turf for sale as well as for their own use. But as the month of July continued wet, the worry grew that the turf would never get dry this summer. The children played through the rainy holidays, Una and Colette, the youngest, slipping out to go visiting along the road or to drop across to Mary's whenever the windows of her kitchen were steamed up with the evidence of fresh scones or a sweetloaf. Often I would leave our own kitchen going down the road with Deirdre and Joseph to Mary's, and find the children gathered there, running around her while she was baking.

Whatever the time of day or evening you are no sooner in Mary's than she offers tea "and a bit of something to go with it."

"No, I won't Mary, I've just had dinner."

"Are you sure, Niall?" Mary says, pausing in midstride across her kitchen, her elbow usually bent and her arm held easily across her front, palm upturned.

"Maybe Deirdre would like a cup of tea and some brown bread?" Mary looks at Deirdre, who sits expectantly at the table, familiar with this routine.

"Deirdre," I say, "would you like something?"

Deirdre nods shyly and answers Mary instead. "Yes, please."

"You'll have a cup of tea, anyway, Niall?"

"All right so, Mary, a cup of tea just," I say, smiling and knowing full well that Mary will also set before me a plate with a knife to spread butter on a slice of her brown bread.

And as the summer moved on, it was in kitchens more than on bogs that the days were spent.

Then, towards the end of July, the drizzle was drawn away like a veil lifted from the green countryside. And the parish moved. From early in the morning there were cars packed with children heading along the Kiltumper road for the Downeses' or Coughlans' bogs. They bumped and rumbled along the road that they only drove at this time of year. "Our annual pilgrims," as one man put it, "coming to get their winter's fuel." For them, Kiltumper only meant one thing: the bog. Many of them came from parishes and villages north of us where there were few or no bogs, or from the sandy soil of the coast, and arrived ten or fifteen miles from home for the day's work, knowing their backs would be aching before they returned to their cars.

The Coughlans' bog runs next to our farm, and machines there cut the turf for over forty families, who back in December have "booked" a "bank," as it were, requesting that P. J.'s machine cut a couple of "hoppers"—the amount of one load—for them. Come summer they must "save" the turf themselves. When the time comes, the turf is spread in long ribbons over the grazing fields, and the now black hillside becomes like a hive as many families set to work footing the sods. From across the fields you can hear the children's voices on the wind. The high stone wall that marks the bounds between our farms screens them, and as I walk up the hill to our own turf there it is, this turf talk, with snippets of conversations, exclamations, and instructions blowing about on the breeze.

The turf that Michael Donnellan cut for us had been footed one dry morning in late June when two of Chris's brothers, Joe and Regis, and Joe's three young daughters were here. We had all marched to the bog and set about building *grogans*. Up there on the windy top of Kiltumper, the children, stooping in Wellies and slickers to lift the heavy sodden lumps, became silent. The great emptiness up there, the heathery wildness of it, the give and bounce and suck of the bogland underfoot, the squelch and blackness, were all as foreign to them as anything in Ireland could be. I watched them from the corner of my eye as I worked. What were they thinking, Meghan and Katy, stacking those wet sods on end? Were they thinking of storylike figures, old greatgrandfather Breens, like the Giant Tumper?

One of Joe's *grogans* fell sideways behind him.

"Hey, Dad, yours are falling down!" shouted Meghan, her voice earnest. "Mine are good ones," she said proudly.

"So are mine, aren't they, Uncle Niall?" said Katy, standing up, pulling a wisp of hair from her face.

"Oh, my kids are great bog-builders!!" shouted Joe.

"Thanks be to God," said I, and Regis quietly answered "Amen," as silence fell over the work again.

Wind blew the purple sprigs of heather. The white feathery bog-cotton bowed forward. We bent down and worked some more. That morning the footing of the turf cast a spell of a kind, the silent work bonding us to the place and to each other. When we moved toward the end of the stacked turf and looked back across the bank at the rows upon rows of standing sods, there was the deepest satisfaction of not only getting the work done, of getting finished what would have taken me so much longer alone, but something more than that, too. Fuel was being won from nature in an ancient way. We were in our own *meithel,* the Irish word used to describe the teams of neighboring men and women who in previous years shared the labor of turf or hay, completing the work of one farm before moving on to a neighbor's.

That afternoon on the phone I told Paddy Cotter that I had had my visitors up footing our turf with me. At first he hadn't believed me.

"Oh yes," I told him, "they footed the lot of it."

"And weren't you a terrible man for putting them to it and the fine day."

"Not at all, Paddy," I said, "wasn't I giving them a memory?"

He exploded with laughter on the other end of the line. "Oh yes," he hooted, "and God knows we have plenty more memories for 'em if they'd care to come down this way."

"Couldn't we make a business of it, Paddy?" I suggested.

"We could," he giggled. "You do our turf, we'll give you the memory. Your back will remember it, your fingers'll remember it . . ."

I, of course, had only been half-joking but when I was

back up on the bog alone, the visitors long gone, it was I who was doing the remembering. A month of almost unbroken rain had meant that the turf was far behind its drying time and needed to be footed once more. And I wished for the aid of Chris's family again as, on another windy day, I headed up across the fields, over the stone walls, to where the turf had been footed into *grogans* by our *meithel*. Some of them had fallen, many lay in puddles that had sprung beneath them, dark and glassy and turning the ends of the sods into a kind of soft wet smulch. Systematically, beginning on the northern edge of the bank and moving slowly southwards, I knocked down the *grogans* of a month earlier, took the sods, and rebuilt them on dry patches of the bank, turning each of them over so the wet ends stood into the air and the work of the *meithel* was literally turned upside down.

As I squatted there, slowly remaking the stacks, I was aware of an extra presence now, tangible and real, in each sod of turf. In some of them it was fingerprints themselves, holes where my godchild Meghan's thumb or finger had pressed clear into the buttery blackness, holes now crusted and hardened into the fuel itself. Memory marks. Presences lingered there on the bogland. For there nothing changed, nothing happened. The turf, besides its documented faculty for preserving fallen trees, bodies of men, or churns of butter, has about it this natural wonder. There, stooping and toiling with me in the silence and the birdsong, was a company of remembered helpers.

I worked on in the silence, losing myself in the simplicity of the work. Up there on the bog of Kiltumper was a hushed agelessness, peopled with memories, the hands that turned and won the turf. As I knocked another *grogan* and it fell

sideways on the heather with a soft sigh, there was Michael
Donnellan with his woolen hat and his *slean,* there were Joe
and Regis and the children, and the people before us, Chris's
cousins and family, her grandfather and his, too, back into
the memory and life of that same place where the wind blew
over the bare banks of the turf and the figures going home
over the stone walls and down the hill fields to the cottage
had the same sense of having handled in summer the life of
another winter, of having stopped time.

I call the huge black shiny plastic-wrapped bales of silage
"art in the landscape." At the end of July the long meadows
down in the valley are pockmarked with them: a hundred
glistening fat slugs in the rain. All over Clare they are neatly
gathered together into corners of fields and wired off from
nosing cattle. The plastic is so thin that the bales have to be
wrapped several times in order to completely seal them. But
even so they are still easy prey for the crows.

The bales glisten and beckon and, like black sitting ducks
in a green pond, the crows descend. Their beaks and talons
puncture the plastic and ruin the silage. In order to deter the
menacing crows, the farmers—and probably the children of
farmers—take to painting in the middle of their summer
chores. The house paintbrush and bucket of white paint are
taken into the field where the fun begins. Huge faces, some

with upturned smiles, others with downturned frowns, some with crooked eyes, some with no eyes, are painted on the tops of the bales. It's art in the landscape and a farmer's secret creativity can let loose: White paint and black plastic become his medium.

On one group of bales, I saw random, single letters painted like a scattered alphabet gift wrapping. And somewhere between Ennistymon and Lisdoonvarna is painted a message: I HATE CROWS, or was it COWS? I was driving too fast to see.

Wrapped silage has quickly become the norm. Prayers are no longer required from the altar for a nice dry spell to cut and save the hay. Now hay can be saved anytime—if the weather is bad, no bother, just call the silage baler. But when the silage is gone, the plastic is left, long thin entrails of black whirring about in the wind, catching on whitethorn and blackthorn, draping a yellow gorse bush like a tattered black evening dress. I know it makes life easier for the small farmers who are struggling to keep going against all odds. The weather is the least of their worries now. And when next summer I see the black leftovers I will remember our own art in the landscape.

We don't need a Christo to wrap our fields; we do it ourselves.

Hardly two days in summer pass now without a visitor. They are all readers. They come into the village and stop in at Michael Fitzpatrick's or ask directions from Gregory at the post office. Even before they ask, it's known where they're heading, and the well-rehearsed directions to Kiltumper are given out.

Gregory has asked me if I would put up a sign.

"To what?" I asked him. "To our house?"

"Well, that's what they all want to see. That's where they're all going. It'd save 'em, a lot of 'em, getting lost, I'd say."

Several times each week we see people going past the house on the lower road, or we're asked by people in the village: "Did ye have Yankees yesterday?" when no one had in fact showed up. There are also Germans coming now as our books have begun to appear in German translation. The number of people losing themselves on the way to Kiltumper has grown considerably. But a sign? It seems all wrong to me, too strange. It is true, it could be argued, we invited visitors. We had made no attempt to disguise the place we lived in; ours was not a fictional landscape, and although in writing about it we had necessarily touched the place with our imaginations, it was real. It was right here. We wrote about our lives as they happened. But it seemed to me that once we put up a sign saying THIS WAY TO KILTUMPER COTTAGE we were turning ourselves into a kind of museum. With a sign up, we would surely feel the pressure of performing, of acting as living examples of ourselves. As if, truly, our life was an invention.

No, the sign seemed completely wrong to me and to Chris. For while we don't mind visitors who come stooping in through the overhanging roses or strolling slowly up the winding garden path, we do often feel a sense that their imagined place was never the destination they arrived at.

When the sun is shining, the garden is an extraordinary place, a little like paradise. And when the weeds have been pulled and the plants deadheaded and the grass cut, it even looks as if it were there for display. But the fact is that, like the rest of our life, it is a living, changing thing. Just as visitors might arrive in a kitchen scattered with children's toys, piled with damp laundry brought in from a rain shower or the tea things uncleared, so too the garden is sometimes ragged and overgrown, wild and falling over, sometimes the plants overgrow the beds, crowd others, mass into tangles of color, choking each other in their struggle for light. More often than not it looks barely under control. And the readers, arriving with their own secret gardens, their Kiltumpers of the mind, might easily be disappointed.

Still, through the summer the visitors come. Many of them bring gifts and some buy Chris's sketches. They come up the garden path under bright umbrellas and stand at the front door saying: "You don't know us, but we know you," or "We're from America." They come from Iowa or California as often as from Boston or New York. What exactly do they come for? I am not sure. But they say it is to see the cottage or the garden, simply to wish us well, or to drive around the Kiltumper roads and see for themselves the places we have written about. They come to tell us of their Irish ancestors or their dreams to move full-time into a cottage in the Irish countryside as Chris and I had done. They ask, What do we think? They come, like a microcosmic emigration in reverse, in search of something for which they feel a deep and sincere need. This alone is certain: Their feelings are genuine and cannot be treated carelessly. In some way we owe it to them.

So, without a sign, and with their cars crawling slowly along the roads from the village, getting lost, passing by the high, often unkempt, hedge in front of the house, going down and around and stopping again and again for directions that as often as not they don't quite understand or remember or match with the curve of broken road they find themselves on, visitors keep arriving at the cottage. Chris and I work on in the summer garden with the children coming and going around the house or standing down by the seven-barred gate waiting when they hear a car.

"Visitors, Daddy!" Deirdre will cry out, jumping from the swing that hangs from the high sycamore to come running with the news, with Joseph leaping along in his Wellies behind her in imitation.

As we know people will be coming throughout the summer, should we in some way prepare for them? To what degree is our private life a public affair? And where is the line of our responsibility, if any, to the Irelands of the mind these people bring with them? This, I feel is something that is applicable on a much larger scale to Ireland in general.

There is an understanding in Ireland that tourism is one of the country's main industries. Ireland depends upon it, and among our attractions as a nation is the friendliness of the people. Indeed, government brochures advertise the people in the same way they speak of the Cliffs of Moher or the Lakes of Killarney.

From time to time there have even been instructions given on television, small timely reminders of what we as a people could do to be helpful to visitors throughout the summer. I remember a man closing a program with a little warning to be on the lookout over the summer for tourists poring over maps at small country crossroads, assuring us that we should not hesitate to go up and offer advice and directions. His warning was hardly needed. The countryside remains as friendly today as it has ever been. We are a people, it seems, who enjoy leaning into car windows, looking curiously at new maps of the island, before disregarding them with a narrowing of an eye, a gaze ahead down the road, and a flurry of instructions to pass on by Nolan's there and beyond the cross and the little bridge and the road in to the left; ignore that, pass on pass on, and shortly you'll be there. And although there have been stories of some tourists getting mugged in Dublin or Cork during the summer, by and large, the country remains extraordinarily welcoming to visitors.

In this context it seems that we should welcome these strangers arriving at *our* door. And welcome them we do, as best we can through these less than summery days of July and August. Joseph and Deirdre are becoming used to people in bright clothes with white sneakers and white teeth uncurling out of rent-a-cars and photographing the hens, and I imagine for them it will seem in time a part of the magic of their childhood here, this procession of foreigners arriving out of the blue, knowing their names, and sometimes bearing gifts.

The arrival of people from Germany is more extraordinary. High-loaded RVs crawl between the hedgerows of the Kiltumper road, bearing mountain bikes strapped on their backs as they resolutely inch along the mucky way to pull up outside Nancy's stable. They come from Berlin, from Bonn, from Frankfurt, the backs of their big vans plastered with insignia and place names, tokens or minor trophies of the journey that has brought them across Europe to us here. Often our visitors' English is fragmentary. Our dialogue is as bizarre and broken as that of explorers meeting natives on some undiscovered shore.

"Mr. Vill-Yams?"

"Yes."

"You write this book? Ya?"

"Ya . . . I mean yes, yes. We . . . Where have you come from?"

Smiles, nods, "Germany."

"Yes, yes, whereabouts?"

The wife turns to the husband, translates, smiles, he smiles back, we all nod at each other, and they tell us where they are from. We stand about a few more minutes. They look out over the garden and the valley and nod their heads and smile, and then give us strong warm handshakes. These alone translate feeling, and we know that we have come to have some kind of special meaning for these complete strangers. They are not Irish, their grandfathers did not emigrate from here, nor did they grow up hearing Irish songs or marching on St. Patrick's Day. For them our life in Kiltumper has another meaning. Ours is the life they are not living: the man and woman and children in the countryside, emblems of a simple way of life they feel they have lost or never enjoyed. It does not seem to matter that they come from well-paid jobs and have their material needs met, while we are constantly on the brink of bankruptcy, wondering how we will continue to survive here. What seems to matter to all of our visitors is that we have done it, that we are *still here.*

✦ Nine ✦

Shannon Airport was opened almost fifty years ago as part of a government policy to develop the West by establishing a duty-free zone and hub of enterprise here. Through a series of government incentives and intense marketing, the region quickly established itself, attracting many international companies. They set up factories and provided much-needed employment opportunities for the people of Clare and Limerick. Shannon town sprung up around the airport.

As well as developing Shannon Airport and the region, the government of the day—a Fianna Fail government—ordained that all transatlantic flights in or out of Ireland had to land first at Shannon. This decision, giving the airport a special status, has caused much debate in Dublin down through the years. To fly from Dublin to New York means a stopover of an hour or so in Shannon, and on returning, a dawn landing—and delay—of many disgruntled Dublin passengers eager to get on across the country to their homes. The effect of the policy for Shannon, however, was and is enormously beneficial. The airport has grown considerably, providing steady employment in Clare and has become one of the success stories of the region. It is the hub of the Shannon region's development with a wide range of service industries growing steadily around it. The tourism industry in the area has become increasingly stronger, with hotels and B&Bs springing up along the roads that lead from the airport into the scenic West. A great majority of American tourists disembark at Shannon Airport from a flight that is going on to Dublin, and everything from car rental companies to restaurants in Clare and Limerick have grown and profited accordingly.

This policy has shown the people of Clare, Limerick, Galway, and the other western counties that the Dublin government was standing behind them, recognizing and supporting the special needs of the West. In granting special status to the airport, the government has really been recognizing the "special status" of the West itself. With the drift of population from the western counties to the urban centers it seems that without special regional policies and assistance the West will decline completely. The "farmers dole"—a weekly social welfare payment in recognition of the unchanging long-term unemployed status of the small farmer—and government grants for cattle—up to £100 a head—which make it possible for families to stay on the land, are a response to this; measures, I know, that many people in Dublin strongly object to (not least the civil servants, who, by and large, through high taxes, feel *they* are supporting the grant schemes and see the payments to farmers as grossly undeserved).

There has always been a sense of division in Ireland between East and West, or rather between the capital and the rural communities. It is rooted in history. From time to time references to "the Pale"—the region around Dublin in which English dominion was most firmly established centuries earlier—come up in partisan speeches in the West. There is, I suppose, a very real fear of the countryman's voice not being heard in Dublin, paradoxical though this seems since the city has grown due to the influx of people migrating from the country.

In October of last year, a month before the general election, and after a long period of pressure for change from a Dublin lobby, the then transport minister for Fianna Fail, Maire Geoghegan-Quinn, announced the government's "absolute endorsement" of Shannon's special status. This, she said, was long-term and unambiguous. That night there were celebration parties in Shannon. If you lived in Clare you felt something genuine had been won. But as the *Clare Champion* later reported: "The watchdogs of the powerful Dublin lobby may have been held at bay but instead of skulking off to lick wounds, new tactics were adopted, influential new allies were cultivated, and an incessant campaign of chipping away at Shannon and the west of Ireland was relentlessly pursued." It was the language of war.

In January 1993, with the new coalition government in place, the question of Shannon was again raised. Aer Lingus was losing money heavily and by early spring this loss was announced to be over a million pounds a week. A rescue plan for the company was linked again with a change in Shannon's status. Dr. Bhamjee and the Labor Party had committed themselves totally to the Shannon gateway and its role in economic development before the election, but the party had also won new North Dublin seats in constituencies around Dublin Airport. Now the Shannon stopover was spoken of as the principal cause of the airline's decline. Aer Lingus was said to be losing passengers to London, who flew there and then back to Dublin rather than be forced to make the one-hour stopover in Shannon.

The new minister, Brian Cowen, ordered the chairman of the airline to prepare a survival plan. It provided for the abolition of the special status at Shannon. There would be no direct flights from Shannon to America for eight months of the year. Aer Lingus's hotels would be sold off, and over 1,500 workers were to be made redundant. Furthermore, it was threatened that if the government forced the airline to continue to land all transatlantic flights at Shannon, then the airline would cease to operate the transatlantic route altogether by the autumn.

There was an expected furor in the West. The western newspapers screamed, and called on the region's elected members of the government to strongly oppose the plan.

By the first week of July it became clear that the government had decided to accept the plan and end Shannon's status. On July 6, the Clare deputy, Tony Killeen, announced he had no choice but to resign from Fianna Fail over what he considered the government's betrayal of the people of Clare. Sile De Valera, the second Fianna Fail member for the region, and a granddaughter of the party's founder, Eamon De Valera, also resigned.

Dr. Moosajee Bhamjee did not resign. In a statement to the papers he declared that he was voting with the government to accept the Aer Lingus rescue plan, and would "play a vital part with his colleagues in government in ensuring that the interests of the Shannon area are given the attention and support required over the coming years." It was, as I was told in Kilmihil that evening, a psychiatrist's response. He didn't "lose his head" over it. What he lost, however, was personal credibility in the eyes of many of the people who had voted for him. "The Labor Party, as the fella says, is always wrestling with its conscience—and winning." But when Tony Killeen arrived back from Dublin at Shannon Airport he was greeted like a hero and carried shoulder-high from the plane.

FINAL BETRAYAL was the headline in the *Clare Champion*. "The government's long-term commitment to Shannon lasted exactly 251 days," said the editorial. "Some commitment. Some government."

Passions were running high. Dr. Newman, the bishop of Limerick, said it was time Dublin realized that the country as a whole did not accept metropolitan domination, that "for any representative of the Pale to seek to do so would be at their peril. We in rural Ireland have put up with enough. How ironic it is that the same country should be seeking eight billion pounds in regional funds from the EC for peripheral areas while ignoring regionality in its own boundaries!"

Along the potholed and broken road of Kiltumper this

evening our sense of loss is strong. There are still to be flights directly to and from Shannon in the summertime. The tourism industry must try to cope and survive; the region must try to market itself more actively now. It is not only fear of the West's economic collapse with the changing of the airport's status that has brought such dismay to the people of Clare. Their feelings are feelings of abandonment by Dublin. The isolation feels that much more intense now.

We throw ourselves into our life on the farm, into life inside the garden hedges, and let the world turn a while without our thinking of it. This spring and summer more than ever before I have been struck with how beautiful the garden is. At last it has begun to take its long-awaited shape with a new curving bed inside the gate and the herbaceous border extended adjacent to the cabins. When you sit on the bench in front of the house there is a near and a far view. Within the high fuchsia hedges in May and June particularly, there is a splash of color—so many reds and yellows, poppies and lupins and anchusa—that contrasts strongly with the world beyond the hedges, where we see the wide view of the valley, rising softly like a series of green blankets on a waking figure. In the distance the road into Kilmihil is evident only when the top of a school bus or tractor passes along it, gliding silently in dreamlike slow motion. The stillness of the valley beyond the high hedge borders the garden with peace. The old bare stone of the cabins runs all down the western side, supporting climbing roses and giving shelter; on the opposite side, past the holly tree and the two ancient, mazy, and twisted sycamores, is the little field where the well is, the

Grove. When you are in the garden with the house behind you, the cabins down the right-hand side, the Grove to the left, and the valley opening out in front of you, you are in a kind of haven. Once, hearing people praise the garden, I had treated the reaction lightly and assumed it was simply a mixture of politeness and the reaction of visitors from abroad to the foreignness of an Irish country garden. Now I have changed my mind.

But Chris would say, smiling, "Look at the weeds," or "But the forsythia is overtaking the border," or "The poppies fell over in the June rain." They had, their flower heads bigger than my two hands, shading everything that was trying to grow beneath and around them. All this is true, of course. But somehow this summer, even as the season itself seemed to lose track of the sun and turned out day after day of pale and washed gray, none of that mattered to me. I was not the gardener Chris was. My eye did not see the things hers did. My lot was to cut the grass and dig the beds and bring the barrows of dung or compost and pull the weeds and move the great overgrown things that needed new neighborhoods; hers to watch and survey, and prune and plant and plot the progress of the whole thing. This year, as I walked around after Joseph, or paused in working on the edge of a bed, I took the time to look around and marvel. For this garden perfectly reflected our life in Kiltumper, nine-plus years, all the springs and summers of our hands' working in this plot of earth before the house.

In the winter, Chris had done a series of drawings: plants to be moved, new paths, and borders. Gardening on paper was part of her therapy for surviving the dark days, and she could spend the entire evening by the turf fire, a stack of gardening books on the floor and numerous sheets of paper with swirls and curves and patterns that were walkways and beds and islands drawn out on them. Among the plans this spring was to break through the wall along the Grove and extend a walkway into the field from the flower garden. Through there, she said, we could have the vegetables and create a long view eastward to where we hoped to plant new apple and pear trees and fruit bushes, and, eventually, the plastic tunnel greenhouse that would be the only certain way of increasing our homegrown food supply.

So this spring I had dug the plot with the help of young Tommy Kilkenny. We planted ridges of potatoes, the American sugar snap peas Deirdre loves, bush beans, onions, leeks, brussels sprouts, and carrots. For ten days in April the sun shone. There was talk of the long hot summer Ireland gets every ten years or so, and that by all calculations we were due one this year. The days were glorious and blue and went down in red evening skies over the sea. In the garden in such weather you planted with a sense of hope and faith and felt the nurturing bond between man and nature.

And then the weather turned cold. The wettest May in memory poured down and three sowings of carrot seed failed to produce a single plant. The peas germinated after the second sowing, and then stopped growing altogether. The same with the beans. The plants simply did not move in the soil. They waited, like us, for the heat and the sunshine. When they did not come, and the days of early June failed to lift the drizzle, the vegetables sat still. Only the onions grew. By Midsummer Day Chris's winter drawings and plans were bearing less and less resemblance to reality beyond the wall in the Grove.

Then the bean plants were attacked by something. Slugs were at the lettuces, and so Chris laid out saucers of old beer between the heads and in the mornings drew out the drunk-dead swollen bodies and pitched them for the crows. The night rains, however, thinned the beer, and after a week the slugs seemed to come and go from the saucer-breweries quite merrily, sated, alive, and thriving. Chris, in a fit, poured salt on a captive and watched as he shrivelled and died; a week later she cut one through with the secateurs in anger and left it out like a warning on a stone. Still the onslaught continued, and as the promise of the summer weakened and the combination of clouds and drizzle spoiled the hope of July, it seemed the garden would yield little but potatoes and onions. The beans were being cleaned to the stalks no matter what we did, and one evening when I was out weeding the destroyed bed I imagined I had found the culprits, hearing the small chirrup sound of a cluster of young pheasants in the long grass beneath the blackthorn hedge. Do pheasants like beans? Perhaps, I thought. But if the beans were lost to us it was better to imagine they were won by the new pheasants than by the slugs or the crows. The pheasants, after all, had been our welcome visitors, and come the autumn we were still hoping to help them survive the Gun Club.

Only half-jokingly did we say that we could never leave Kiltumper—not because of the house but because of the garden. Work on and in the garden had become an unquestioned part of our life. The garden was a retreat, a place to be alone with yourself. In the garden was both stillness and action, soul and body. And when the news of the bigger world—heart-wrenching Somalia or Bosnia, a school-friend's death, family illness—broke into the cottage in Kiltumper, leaving a heavy knot of grief and helplessness, we could go outside and sit and stare down the still valley, go down on our knees and pull weeds.

While immigration to America is a fact of life throughout the smaller rural towns and villages in Ireland, nowadays it is not always a matter of necessity. There are many young Irish people who have grown up in depressed rural areas, on small farms, who cannot wait to leave the land. Some of them, seeing no future in farming, witnessing the struggles of their parents to keep the farm going and feed and raise the children, develop a kind of rural sense of inferiority, a loathing of being seen as countrified. For the young, listening to international rock music and watching television programs from America, England, and Australia, the thing to look like in Kilmihil is anything but a countryman. They aspire to be like the tanned and easy teenagers of American television series. Going to America is for many not so much an enforced sentence of exile as an opportunity for escape. What the young rural Irish person wants to be is *American*.

It is not uncommon to see children in Kilmihil wearing clothes sent home from a brother or sister in America, going about the village in Boston Red Sox or Chicago Bears sweatshirts. The Irish clothes shops pick up this taste, and even for small children of two, such as Joseph, offer baseball-type tracksuits and high-top sneakers. During the summer you will see farmers on their tractors more frequently wearing baseball caps now than the traditional cloth ones.

If there has been a mainstay in the realm of clothing fashions for farming communities, it is a preference for deep and dark colors, grays and browns and greens. There is a traditional aversion to showiness. When I saw a middle-aged bachelor driving his tractor wearing a bright red sweater and loud checked jacket, it was explained to me with a knowing look, "They were a present from America." (I, myself have frequently encountered a disappointed response to my own appearance from visitors who felt my khaki trousers and T-shirt were disappointingly not "Irish-looking" enough.)

But we often meet readers who visit the cottage, who were born and have lived all their lives in America, who feel they are and want in some passionate way to be *Irish*. It was just this strangely entangled relationship between Ireland and America that I wanted to explore when I wrote *The Murphy Initiative*. I had lived now on both sides of the Atlantic and felt the opposing pressures and tugs of the different nationalities. As a Dubliner I had never felt more Irish than when in New York. And although I looked like any other young copywriter walking up Park Avenue and across West Fifty-Seventh Street, I had brought to the office my nationality. My accent was remarked on as "having a lilt" though I didn't for a moment think it had. Indeed, when I returned "home" to Dublin during those years, my mother often teased me that I had now "a bit of a twang." In the wealth and affluence of Upper Westchester County, where Chris and I were neither wealthy nor affluent, being Irish was a form of escape. I clung secretly to my country no matter how I seemed to be fitting into the life of America. I visited the Irish bookshop downtown, went to see the Northern Irish film *Cal* on my lunch break, and continued to devour the works of Irish writers I admired.

Coming from Dublin and not one of the tightly knit and

interconnected parishes in the West, I did not have a network of emigrated friends, neighbors, or relations like so many of those I see leaving Clare. I did not go to Gaelic Park or to hear the Clancy Brothers at Carnegie Hall, even as I had not when in Dublin. Instead my sense of Irishness was internally fed almost entirely through literature. I read Yeats on my break from writing copy for some new romance novel.

For the boys and girls in my class their experience of America will not be the same as mine. They will go to Queens or Yonkers, to Glover, Maclean and Hyatt Avenues. Like Maura Dooley, Michael and Breda's daughter. Or like Rita Callinan, who was in our drama group. To the Rumours Pub in Yonkers, to cousins and friends already there, with jobs in construction or nannying and rooms already lined up. In a way they will go to the New Kilmihil, the other Kilmihil out there, which is like the shadow of this one—or perhaps it is this one that is the shadow now. News of Clare and of Kilmihil football matches will be known in their local pub no later than the final whistle. Videos will be on the way, and parish rivalries and loyalties will be no less passionate for being three thousand miles away. They will keep up with news of funerals and marriages, one phone call from home letting out the spore of village news that will travel around and through the transatlantic community, so that in The Bronx they will know all about exam results at home or marriages and the style of the wedding dress. And although in the greater openness of American society they may miss mass more frequently, cook and bake less, they too will cling to a sense of being Irish. It is not surprising that many of the Irish national *feiseanna*, traditional step dancing or music competitions, are won in Ireland by visiting

American-born children of Irish parents. These are the same parents who, when they were in school, growing up in rural western Ireland, had time only for pop and rock and roll. American and Ireland are bound together now, raising for us the question: Are we really on the western periphery of Europe? Or is this the far eastern coast of the United States?

This summer Ireland celebrated the thirtieth anniversary of the visit here of John F. Kennedy. The arrival of Kennedy in Ireland in 1963 was one of those moments in the country's history that had since taken on the quality of legend. There was a sense of epic gesture in the handsome president's return to his ancestral home in Wexford. On the anniversary of the occasion this year RTE broadcast several hours of old black-and-white footage of the visit. There was pathos, with the knowledge of tragedy later that same year, but also, watching it this year in its entirety—the crowds of admirers following him around, the innocence, the generosity and welcome pressed upon him, town mayors making speeches with tears in their eyes—what struck me most was the symbol he had offered us, the positive side of all that emigration, the dazzling smile of highest achievement. President Kennedy was not beyond playing the occasion for what it was worth. As he approached "a family tea" at his ancestral home, now Mrs. Ryan's, he waved forward toward the cameras the crowds of farmers and their families who were at the end of the road, out of view, waiting just for a glimpse of him. They came like sheep in a pack down the road. Some of the men took off their caps, and for a moment he looked like *their* returned son.

Success shone off him, and in a way I could understand how any mother or father grieving over the loss of a child to

Boston or the Bronx might have gazed at the president and felt the hope: Sure, in America there's plenty work, that's the place to be. Sure, what is there here for them? Couldn't they become whatever they wanted in America? When Kennedy addressed the crowd in Wexford and wondered what might have happened if his grandfather had not left Ireland, and said perhaps he'd be working today for the Albatross Company, whose sign was displayed on a building across the road, the crowd laughed; laughing, as the journalist Fintan O'Toole has pointed out, in some ways at themselves and what seemed such ordinary, rural, even backward lives next to his.

While Kennedy came here as an Irishman, it was his American qualities that so attracted us.

When *The Murphy Initiative* was staged in Dublin, it sought to bring together the two sides of this entangled relationship in a dramatic and comic way. On the one hand were two young Irish characters who dreamed only of being Americans, whose images of America were derived largely from a diet of Western movies and who lived in West Clare as if on some western plain of the imagination, who in their own eyes were rustlers and outlaws, after a fashion. On the other hand was an American character, visiting what he thought was his grandfather's ancestral home, a man thoroughly versed in Irish literature who took from it his own images of what Ireland should be like. The truth was that both country's images were only that, creations of the mind.

A few evenings ago, the news came that Digital, a computer company based in Massachusetts, was considering cutting back on its European operations. The rumor that the Galway plant, with over a thousand workers, was under threat sent shock waves up and down the western coastline. Ruari Quinn, the minister for employment and enterprise, flew to Boston to argue the case for the west of Ireland, and returned "hopeful."

Meanwhile, Galway waited. But following weekend meetings at Digital headquarters it was announced that eight hundred workers in Galway are to be laid off. There is loss and gloom in the air, for those who live on this side of the country know only too well how few are the industries and enterprises offering employment here on the furthest edge of Europe.

In the same evening news, on a note that would be surrealistic were it not so sadly real, we hear that for a hundred new jobs in Cork, there have been nine thousand applications.

Tonight we load the turf high on the fire that burns every night of the year on our hearth in Kiltumper and sit a little closer while the children sleep.

✦ TEN ✦

It seems that if the West is to survive it will do so not because of some sudden change in the economic viability of farming, nor even because of the bestowal of local employment by foreign industries, but because of the "blow-ins," those who have come from elsewhere and truly chosen to make a life in the rural communities. Such people bring with them an appreciation of what the countryside has to offer without feeling the pessimism or sense of entrapment of some who have never left. New settlers bring new energy to the area. I don't just mean people with holiday homes along the scenic western seaboard, or the summer influx in the seaside towns. Of course they, too, count. But the summer season in the west of Ireland is only two months long, and the ruggedness of the weather along the rain-washed and wind-swept coast guarantees that from September to June the tourist shops and cafés are closed, and by and large miss little in the way of business. But there are couples, some with small children, who are now choosing to leave a largely urban lifestyle and settle in the countryside. This is a scattered phenomenon at the moment; families leave the cities for their own reasons and make new homes where they choose.

But on the Loop Head peninsula at the end of West Clare, a sculptor, Jim Connolly, established the Rural Resettlement Scheme as a direct answer to the drastic depopulation of the area west of Kilkee. He made an appeal to families—especially those unemployed—in Dublin to pack up and move down to Clare, where, even if they continued to be unemployed, they would at least be sure of a better, healthier lifestyle and a safer environment for their children. What's more, if they had some trade or skills they would be certain to find use for them in a place where services were running down. He asked the people of Clare to make available at cheap rates for settlers some of the many vacant old cottages.

To date, the scheme has settled over a hundred families in different parts of the West, and Jim Connolly and his team have received awards and considerable national and international attention. Some families, of course, did not transplant well; they found the countryside too bleak in winter, too quiet, no cars passing, the people too clannish and settled. Or they missed their apartments or the old neighborhood, however much they had complained about them before. But still, a growing number have stayed.

In our own townland of Kiltumper *we* were blow-ins of a kind, as were Jim and Kay up the road. There is an English lady down the road and an English man from Chelsea further out in the old cottage at the head of the valley. Each of us is a bringer of change—active or passive—to the community. If you sit in the conservatory—the first and only one so far in the townland—that Jim and Kay have built at the front of their cottage and look out through the pergola down to the rose garden and the big plastic tunnel where their cucumbers and tomatoes are growing, you must see a renewal of the possibilities here. The influence of these new people will eventually bring new ways of thinking about life here—about being enterprising and looking forward, about possibility and richness and a value for a life that is available in these rural townlands.

All of this came to mind as we were driving down to Kerry in the first week of July to see Bonnie. Bonnie had phoned us from New Jersey five years ago when she read our first book and was considering moving to the west of Ireland. The place she had blown into—Slea Head at the end of the Dingle peninsula—is one of the most beautiful in the country. And there, with her mother, Margaret, she had taken over the Slea Head guesthouse. It was an extraordinary move in many ways—the guesthouse is right in the heart of the West Kerry Gaeltacht; her neighbors are Irish speakers; it is miles out from Dingle and away from the busiest corner of the tourist route; it is the only guesthouse of its kind out there at the bend in the road where the Great Blasket Island appears like a green wedge off the shore. Bonnie was already near fifty when she moved. It didn't seem the kind of decision that could really work; surely, after a year or two at most, the churning of those winter seas, the mists and the dark and the wind and rain, the sheer *foreignness* of the place would get to her and she would be forced to return to Cape May, New Jersey.

Not so. Bonnie has stayed. And at Christmastime every year she sends us one of the teddy-bear calendars she and her son Chris make, as if marking ahead the resolve to stay on another year.

We had been down to visit her only once in four years. This summer, with Chris's brother Joe and his wife and children, we decided there were few better destinations to head for. So we made the fabulous drive over the Conor Pass and into Dingle once again, between the green mountains coming down to the sea, the car moving along the curving roads as the water rushed down the hill fields, gushing in rivulets, racing for the Atlantic.

Even in the broken weather Dingle town was busy. We drove on out towards Slea Head, losing cars, people, and houses, as we wound along the sea road. There is an atmosphere of leaving things behind that you can almost feel in the road itself. The traffic for generations has been all one way—the other direction—as the people of the three Blasket Islands gradually left. Drifting away from the headland, men, women, and children went back, eastwards along the outreached finger of the penninsula, first to Dingle, and from there into the world.

Beyond Ventry the road is an outpressed lip above the moody ocean. The gray crags of the hillside on the right cut sharply into the road as it bends about them, going on, further and further west, relentlessly seeking an end, across the place where a mountain stream crosses the road and falls away through a hole cut in the stone parapet down into the sea, on past the grotto built into the mountain with the white crucifix and the Blessed Virgin gazing out across the water. On and on, this westerly road seeks an end, and finally finds it round the bend at Slea Head.

The view alone stops you. There is a feeling of pilgrimage about arriving.

We drove on another fifty yards and came to Slea Head house and saw—teddy bears! The house, an old two-story building looking out to the islands, had been painted a dark brownish gray as a backdrop for a large mural of teddy-bear scenes. The bears were everywhere: They rose from painted shrubbery, one of them held out his paw, another peeked around a WELCOME sign, two more were hanging off a crescent moon. They were jolly and cheerful and childlike and as unlikely as anything you could imagine in the center of the traditional West Kerry Gaeltacht.

At first I was so surprised, I didn't know what I thought of them. The children stared up at the fantastic bear house where they were going to stay. Inside, the house was as we had remembered it, simple and restful, with Irish music playing always and rooms looking out onto the green slope of the Great Blasket Island. After a moment Bonnie appeared to welcome us; five years in Slea Head hadn't changed her in the slightest. We stood in the sitting room before the spectacular view, and as the children ran outside to study the teddy bears, she told us she still had no regrets.

"It's hard sometimes, you know, to make ends meet." She gave a soft laugh. "But we get by, same as everyone."

Since we had last been there she had opened a tearoom and a small gift shop for handmade cards and Christmas decorations that she and her mother created during the quieter days of autumn.

"You do whatever you can, don't you?" she said. "And we had so many people stopping for the view. Now sit down and I'll bring out some tea and chocolate chips—they still bring them, you know."

It was one of her passions, along with Christmas and cats and teddy bears, and since we had first met Bonnie and written about her, visitors had started coming to Slea Head with bags of chocolate chips for her cookies. She kept the guesthouse open all year and lived within that wintering Atlantic community by making calendars, cards, and Christmas decorations. And she seemed to be thriving on it.

"Well, you need to keep doing something, don't you? I mean,"—she cast her eyes to the heavens—"I'm using eleven cans of cat food a day." She shook her blond head and puffed on her extra-long cigarette.

"And what about the teddy bears?" I said.

"Do you like them? A lot of people don't. Well, some. Some don't, some do. You have to create your own fantasy, don't you? This is my fantasy. That's my fantasy, too, out there." She pointed to the island now being painted in a brilliant wash of sunlight. In the changing weathers it was never the same. On its still fields, rising in a green hump, I could imagine I saw the figures of ghost islanders and their few cattle moving through the stillness.

There was controversy here in West Kerry too. An interpretative center had been planned and built by the OPW near Ballyferriter. The Blasket Islands Interpretative Center, an unattractive-looking building in our eyes, was not yet open but during its construction it had, according to Bonnie, caused wide rifts among the local population. The same arguments that the Mullaghmore Center provoked had arisen here too. There was some local support for an enterprise that would bring employment, and strong opposition from those who felt the project unsuitable and even an insult to the memory of the heroic people of the Blaskets. Here again, in what seems a phase of contemporary Irish development, it was impossible to find a middle ground. There were claims that government was forcing these centers on the local population, moving quickly to utilize ready European funding without due consideration of the full implications, and counterassertions that the centers were the only way to capitalize on tourism and that objections were based on woolly romanticism.

We sat there in the westward-looking room watching the islands' constantly changing weather. I might have sat there all evening, but the children had come inside. They had seen Bonnie feeding a lamb from a baby bottle, they had counted the teddy bears, they had been in the gift shop and seen the great reindeer and the other Christmas things. All of which created a bubbling sense of holiday fantasy deepened by the sudden sunshine and the opening of blue sky over us.

We headed off to the beach, a lovely strand down a curving stairway where the sea crashed on an apron of white sand between the high rocks. Your footprints were like those of Robinson Crusoe, and from that sheltered loveliness between the rocks, the sea tumbling high waves, and the sky cloudless and blue, you never wanted to be rescued. So we played into the late evening sunshine, Joe and Eileen, and Katy, Meghan, and Devon, and Chris and me, and Deirdre and Joseph, each of us daring the others to venture into the freezing cold water. We played Frisbee and baseball and the girls did gymnastics. We felt safe and warm, and the troubles and worries of our lives seemed held just offshore with the clouds.

Walking back toward the house later in the evening I passed a cottage with its front door open to the sea. Nearly out of sight was a peaked cap inside the door peering out.

"The summer's in," I said toward the doorway. Instantly an old man leaned out from his watch and nodded and smiled. "'Tis," he said.

"Have you the hay saved?" I called up to him.

"I haven't," he called happily back across the sunny road.

"Time for it yet," I said, and he nodded and waved a short little wave of his hand toward the sky as if to indicate the heavens would take care of it in time.

"*Slan*," he called down to me and I called it back up to him and walked on, leaving him to settle back into his long silent watch of the sea and the summer evening.

A little further on down the road I met another man in his sixties coming with two empty plastic buckets, dribbles of fresh milk in the bottoms of them. He wore a shabby jacket over his sweater, and his cap angled to the left as he held his head slightly to the right. I greeted him as he got near me and he stopped for a moment to catch his breath, both of us standing there in the easy sunlight on the loop of that magnificent bay, both of us lightened by the weather, the place, the lift of the big sky.

"Great day," I said.

"'Tis." He clicked the word through a gap in his teeth, and after a beat added, "thank God."

"If you've hay to save this'll be the week for it."

"I have that meadow down there," he said with pride, pointing below us to a small narrow field high with hay that ran sharply downward to the very edge of the sea. It was a difficult place to save hay—small, sloping sharply down and away at the same time—and as I looked at it I realized suddenly that it would be cut and saved by hand. There would be no tractor going in that field, no black baled silage there.

"The top'll be dry and the bottom wet, and it'll be falling all the time down before me," he said.

We stood looking down at the treacherous little meadow. He knew it like he knew his face. Perhaps better.

"*An bhfuil Gaelige agat?*" he asked me suddenly, with a note more of hope than interrogation, and with a sudden deepening of intimacy. For, it seemed, if I had the Gaelige, if I could speak Irish, then we could have a proper conversation.

"*Beagan,*"" I answered, wishing that I had more than a little.

But that was enough for him and he was off, speech flowing happily from him in sea waves, telling me of the field, of the hay, of a funny story one time when they were saving it, that was his house above there, with the window, there, yes, that one, and they were at the hay and—he chuckled to himself telling me even as I was losing the story in the rush of his Irish—"*cluckcluck, cluckcluck mar sin,*" and his hand fluttered up in the air becoming a chicken in his story, the chicken he and his brother thought had been taken by the fox, and there as they were saving the hay in that little meadow, they discovered newborn chicks.

"*Ocht, cluckcluck, mar sin,*" he grinned, holding up eight fingers with his thumbs tucked in, flying back into his memory of that moment in his meadow there by the sea. He finished and we stood looking down into the field. I was struck by the simplicity and wonder of the man, how such a day and the discovery of the chicks amidst the hay still gleamed in his memory. He paused a while, then asked me my name.

"*Niall MacLaim. Ta me i mo gconai i Cill Mhicil i gContae an Chlar.*"

"*Cill Mhicil,*" he said, in deeper, richer Irish sounds than mine. "*Tomas O Dalaigh.*" He half-offered his hand, just lifting it ever so slightly into the air between us. It was not an expansive or broad gesture, but it was there nonetheless; something, however fragile, shared though he and I were almost as different as we could be. He had lived his life there in that house above the ring of the bay. He *was* part of the little field across the road as much as the broken wire fence around it; we were different faces of the same country and in the moment in the summer evening we had found gratitude in each other's presence. I shook his hand. It was curved and hard and my fingers within it were in place of pitchfork or shovel or scythe. He asked me where I was staying and when I pointed back across the bend of the road to Bonnie's, he smiled and said in foreign-sounding English, "The teddy bears."

"The teddy bears."

From a hundred yards away the house blended perfectly into the hillside, the bears were gone. It was only as you got nearer that you began to see them. I asked Tomas what he thought of them; after all, he lived only down the road and had known the house before Bonnie arrived there. He shrugged and smiled; it wasn't so important. Some liked it, some didn't. But she was a strong woman, he told me; she was up there on ladders with paint doing all that herself, all day and the next. "That painting's not easy work," he added, "And then of course it brings people." We gazed back at the house.

"She's a strong woman, Bonnie," he repeated, and I had the sense that it was her tenacity, her staying power and inventiveness that impressed him, for he knew what it cost to live through winters in such a place.

We left each other with *slans* and walked home. Between his house and Bonnie's, around the bend of Slea Head, were past and present Irelands, and as I got closer to the guesthouse and could see the teddy bears on the walls I felt no sense of one life threatening the other; rather, it was just such a mingling of the old and new, I thought, that would keep rural places alive.

Half of my family have come for a visit. My father, Joe, and Polly, my stepmother; my brother Regis and his friend Nancy; and my brother Joe and his wife, Eileen, and their three daughters, Caitlan, Meghan, and Devon. We have a full house. Thank goodness we have the new kitchen to accommodate us all. My brothers and father are very tall and with Niall, too, that makes for some big appetites. There are thirteen to feed. You might say that feeding visitors is a preoccupation for the Irish, and even I have got into the habit of being concerned whether there is enough food for everyone. Because if we run short I can't just dash out to the shops. Well, I can, but I mightn't be able to get anything to suit an American's palate. For that I have to go into Ennis and we've been to Abbey Meats, the wonderful gourmet shop there, several times already. Today, my father is looking for capers, and I haven't the heart to tell him that there won't be any in Kilmihil.

We are sort of having a pasta competition in the evenings. (There aren't any restaurants to cater for us in the immediate locality, nowhere to go just to get a quick bite to eat.) So Dad and Regis are taking turns seeing who can outcook the other. They are both terrific chefs— when it comes to pasta, that is. And Polly is delighted with the fresh herbs in the garden and gathers herself a separate bowl each evening to add to her meal. She especially loves the little blue borage flowers. Nancy, Eileen, and I do the dishes. In the morning there are fresh scones and my brother Joe says he loves my brown bread. For our part, Niall and I have tried to create an atmosphere of holiday all around. It might never happen again—this gathering of Breens in Kiltumper—and I want it to be unforgettable. And little Joseph is revelling in the calling of his name. Every time someone calls "Joe," he turns around and smiles. "I'm not Joey," he says, "I'm Joseph. I'm Joseph Daire Breen Williams."

One of the nicest things about their visit is that both my father and my brother Joe are celebrating their birthdays. So we cooked a fourteen-pound salmon. Regis, a seafood connoisseur, stuffed it with lemons and herbs and butter, and we put it in the Aga and waited. Everyone is a little skeptical of the Aga because it has no temperature control, and my American relations, used to microwaves and temperature-controlled cooking, think this big black cast-iron cooker is medieval. Can it cook at all? And how can it possibly taste much better? Is it really worth the trouble? Their answers came, although a bit delayed because of the Aga's temperament, in the shape of a deliciously moist and flavorsome wild Irish salmon.

We sang happy birthday and recalled all the Joseph Breens who had ever been beside the big open hearth. And there were a lot of them, from Joseph, my grandfather, to Joesoe, my father's cousin down the road, to a Joseph Breen in England and one in Australia—all sons of brothers of this house. My father was especially nostalgic because it is his roots that have been reclaimed here in Kiltumper and through our little Joseph, another Joseph Breen will grow to manhood like my father's father, here.

Three weeks after our visit to Bonnie at Slea Head, West Kerry hit the newspaper headlines with a story that put the influence of the new on the old in a different perspective. In Teach Peig, a pub in the Gaeltacht village of Ballyferriter, publican Sylvie O'Connor had been thinking of ways to draw the tourists out from Dingle. He had bought the pub eighteen months earlier when he moved with his wife and daughter from Raheny in Dublin. As the story had it, he had been thinking of organizing set dancing or some similar entertainment when a wag said: Make it topless and you'll draw the crowds. On the first night of the following week, Sylvie had offered £100 to any lady dancing topless. The offer was not taken up. On the second night the offer rose to £200, and so on each night, the money finding no takers until it had risen to £600—at which point there were two, both (depending on who was telling the story) tourists from Dingle. The women danced topless and the pub hit the national headlines as part of the summer silly season.

In Ballyferriter, however, a village of seventeen residents, a Garda station, petrol pumps, post office, a shop, and three other pubs, the locals were up in arms. The parish priest, Father Tomas O'Hiceadh, told his congregation to "stand firm against topless dancing in Ballyferriter." (He was also against Teach Peig hosting a planned blues festival, which he said was totally out of keeping with the tradition and culture of the parish, though he said he was at least willing to live with the music.)

Meanwhile, the controversy bubbles on. There have been allegations of threatening phone calls to the O'Connors. A local committee has been established to formally object to the dancing, and today the news reports that a petition with over a thousand signatures is being sent to the minister for justice, Maire Geoghegan-Quinn, asking her to ban topless dancing. The area, say the locals, is a celebrated Gaeltacht where families send their children every summer to learn Irish. Ballyferriter is no place for bare breasts.

✦ ELEVEN ✦

When I was growing up in Dublin, neither my mother nor my father imagined that I would come to live in a rural parish in West Clare.

By the time I had finished my degree at University College Dublin, in English and French, I wanted nothing more from life than to become a writer. For a time, I suppose, the impracticality of this must have worried my parents greatly—though they did not say so. My mother would only smile and say, "Do the best you can, Niall, that's all."

My father delayed for as long as possible asking me exactly

how I was going to get on in the world. How quickly the country itself must have been changing at that time. It was no longer the place where semi-state bodies could take on great numbers of school-leavers each year, where the old certainties of a post in the bank or the civil service could swallow up great numbers and deliver that thing—the secure job—which took the parents' worry away. My father had joined the Electricity Board as a young man and worked nowhere else all his life. He knew the value of such a life, the disadvantages of not working all those years in the private sector, as well as the pride he felt at being, at its loftiest and lowest, "a public servant."

When I met Chris, left Ireland, and went to America, that aspect of my father's working life kept coming back to me. I had the sense that people such as my father, public servants with a sense of national commitment, people who knew they could have earned more and lived better in other work, were becoming virtually extinct. I identified them and the people of their generation with the Republic, a country just thirty years old in the 1950s; they and Ireland were more closely linked than I or any generation since could be. In the moments in New York when I felt that life as a well-paid copywriter left something missing, it was just that feeling of wanting to be in some way connected to the life of the country that I kept coming back to. It was an unfashionable thing to be thinking in 1982; besides, my constituency was Yeats and Joyce and Synge, and as removed from the real Ireland as anything could be. Still, there it was. My father sent me copies of the *Irish Times*. I kept in touch. And then one week he sent the paper with a government advertisement encircled. The Department of Foreign Affairs was holding national examinations in February toward the recruitment of third secretaries.

For several days I carried the ad back and forth with me on the train into Manhattan. It had come at what seemed a critical time in my life, a time for decisions, a time when I was about to settle down to become an American. Finally, with encouragement from Chris, I sent in the application. My father offered to pay for my flight home to sit the examination. As it happened, it was not necessary. Three weeks later I was informed that I could take the examination in the Irish Consulate offices on Fifth Avenue on the 22nd of March.

That morning as I travelled in on the commuter train from Westchester I was in a way secretly returning home, and I turned off my usual path up Park Avenue with a sense of my footsteps taking me back paradoxically to somewhere I had never been, adult Ireland. I went upstairs and rang the bell. There was no answer. I waited and rang again, and after a while a frowning, flustered man appeared in his coat, looking as if he had just come in through some secret other door, was on the point of undertaking something that required all his concentration, and was a little put out by my interrupting. I introduced myself and showed him my letter. In a Dublin accent he told me to wait and, taking the letter, abruptly disappeared. It was a moment before he opened the door again. His coat was off now and his manner still short and hurried. He was a bald man with a well-fed figure.

"Come in here. Wait there."

The view from the reception room looked down onto Fifth Avenue. An open doorway to one side led to a room with typewriters no one was using. The whole place seemed empty but for the Dublin man with the bald head. He reappeared from the back room, all business and haste, a long envelope in his hand.

"Come this way now," he said and walked over to what appeared to be the wall. A hidden door, or at least one I had not seen, opened in the wall and we stepped into a small dark corridor with offices along it. "In here." He stood back and I entered a long brown room in half-light with venetian blinds pulled closed and the smell of old smoke. There was a long oval-shaped mahogany table and high-backed heavy chairs surrounding it.

"Sit down there," he said, pointing to the far end as he laid down the envelope and a packet of cigarettes on the near one.

I walked over and sat down, took off my jacket, and took out two pens, still just grasping the fact that I was alone in sitting the exam in New York, and that even as I sat there, there were hundreds in Dublin not yet awake who would be going in to one of the centers in the city that morning for the same paper.

"The envelope is sealed," said my examiner in a flat tone. He might have being saying the world is round, or the morning is here, or anything else that occurred to him, his voice was so matter-of-fact, all life drained out of it.

"Sign it, please," he said and got up and carried the envelope down the long table to me. It might have slid nicely on the polished mahogany, I thought, but I signed my name and handed the envelope over.

The examiner went back up to the head of the table opposite me. He sat down, drew out the paper, and put it before him.

"The clock behind me is the official one," he said. "That's the one I'll be using. You are not allowed to bring anything other than a pen into this room. If you have any notes or papers on you, this is the time to remove them." He was not looking at me, he was looking down at the box of his cigarettes. He waited, sighed. "If there is any evidence of cheating I will be obliged to take your paper from you, destroy it, and disqualify you from the examination." He paused. "Is that clear?"

"Yes," I said, thoroughly uncomfortable and with mixed feelings about wanting to be part of the organization this man belonged to.

He stood up. "It is now nine twenty-seven," he said. "You can turn over the paper at nine-thirty."

They were the longest three minutes. I had nothing in front of me and stared down the long table at the bald man who was transfixed by the dust motes above my head. One minute, two minutes. He didn't move, just sat there like an overfilled mailbag, slouched, waiting, as if the slightest communication were so beyond official regulations that should it occur lights would flash on and he would certainly be forced to leave the country.

"You have three hours." And walking down the length of the table again, he laid the paper before me. "The examination has now begun," he said and walked back up the room to the head of the table, drew back his chair, sat down, and lit a first cigarette.

The clock moved in two-minute leaps. Along the wall around us in the dim light were framed pictures of the presidents of Ireland and other national figures, their faces with strong chins staring forward at the visionary country that was now in the past. There was something strangely clashing about the whole business—my examiner with his blank and bland expression sitting at the other end of the table, not reading or moving, smoke rising from him, staring down beyond me at the dust even as the presidents did, and the traffic and noise of Fifth Avenue rising in a din from the street below. It was discomforting.

I looked down at the exam paper, found a question on the role of literature, and started writing. As always, once I was writing, the world went away and I forgot the round man and his smoky dreamgaze of boredom and the presidents and my misgivings on my arrival. I wrote on for three hours, only occasionally hearing the faint noises from the inner office or the voice of an Irish woman in the corridor. The examiner lit cigarettes and smoked, amusing himself for a time with various ways of exhaling into the room. But he did not leave his chair. Fifteen minutes before the three hours were up I had finished writing and could add no more to my answers. I put down my pen and sat there at the far end of the table opposite my examiner. I tried to catch his eye but he looked beyond me.

"There are fifteen minutes left," he said, making it clear by his tone that he would not accept my answer sheet until then. And so we sat there, this man and I, in the Irish Consulate on Fifth Avenue beneath the smoky black portraits of Hyde and De Valera and the rest. The answer sheet on the table, I thought, could turn out to be one of the significant things, a turning point in my life. It was like a passport home, I imagined, not yet disentangling the paradox of going back to Ireland in order to join the Department of Foreign Affairs and be posted abroad. No, at that moment, I was full of a simple desire to succeed in the exam, and sat there on the edge of becoming, like my father, one of the country's civil servants.

The clock ticked on and finally the examiner stood up and walked down to me. He took the manuscript of my answers back up the room and slipped it inside a manila envelope. Then he opened the door and led me out through an office now humming with activity.

"Good-bye now," was all he said, turning with the same expressionless face and heading back in to the typewriters.

I came down into Fifth Avenue exhausted and exhilarated, losing myself in the crowd and heading home early to Mt. Kisco. But even as I sat on the train going home, time and again the face and manner of the man kept coming back at me. How dreadfully unhappy he seemed, how lifeless and gray, and yet had he not one of the plum postings in the world—Fifth Avenue, New York? The examination lay between us like a bridge. If I was successful, I suddenly thought as we passed Chappaqua in the empty train, would I become him? It was an unnerving thought, and I buried it along with my own keen but somewhat childish disappointment that I had not been *welcomed* more, that I had felt no sense of being taken within a community of Irish people living in America.

A couple of weeks later my father called from Dublin and told me he had heard that there were about four hundred or so candidates and the likelihood was that there would only be three positions to be filled. I explained to him that my knowledge of Irish political and business life was weak and that he should not hold out much hope for me in the exam.

"Sure, we'll see," he said, "you did your best, that's all."

It was a month later when I heard. "*A Cara*," said the

letter, using the standard Irish opening (literally, "Friend"). "I am pleased to inform you that you have been successful in your recent examination . . . . Please attend at this office on May 15th for an interview."

Chris and I were both delighted. A globe of possibilities was spinning. For the journey back to Dublin I packed a new gray suit that Chris had bought at Barneys in New York, a white button-down Oxford shirt, and black loafers. They could ask questions in Irish, I had been told, and so I carried on the plane an Irish-English dictionary I had picked up downtown. I tried out words in my head across the Atlantic, Gaelic sounds dropping like islands or stepping stones into the vastness of the way back. A friend inside the department had told me that my score on the examination was one of the highest, and so, exalted by a sense that the third secretaryship was within my grasp, I returned to Ireland expectant and hopeful with an optimism and resolve that I didn't yet realize was American.

It was only on the morning of the interview, when I stood in the hallway at my parents' home, suited and shining, as I had seen my father do for over a quarter of a century, when my mother said, quite casually, "You look very American in that suit, Niall," that the illusion began to fall away. My father drove me into the city on his way to work. It was the only time in my life that we sat together in suits in the morning traffic, like any two civil servants heading in to the paperwork.

But it was not quite so. My father left me and wished me good luck and I headed up O'Connell Street to the interview. Somewhere in the shadows, in the moving crowds heading for the offices, was the figure of the bald and blank-faced examiner from New York. He kept coming into my mind. And I kept dismissing him.

Inside the building where the interviews were taking place a receptionist took the letter I had been told to bring and directed me to sit and wait. Five minutes later a red-faced young man in a brown suit emerged from the interview room. Coming over to get his coat he nodded in my direction.

"How did it go?" I asked.

"Well, I think," he said. "But I've done it before and not got it, so. . ." He shrugged. "Where're you from yourself?"

"I'm from Dublin," I said, a little surprised that he had asked.

"Oh," was all he said, but it was enough to send me fluttering through a catalog of worries about my clothes and accent. Why had I worn a button-down shirt? And the suit, the suit was too elegant, was too *what*? American. (Or so I imagined; button-down shirts had not yet become popular in Ireland, nor the American cut of a suit. No one, I thought, looked like me that morning in Dublin.)

Within, there were three men in three different shades of gray suits. They sat behind glasses of water at a mahogany table and began by asking me what I was doing in America. Their tone was formal, not friendly; mine was suddenly an examined life, under the microscope, being searched for certain qualities or characteristics from which third secretaries could be made. I tried to answer clearly and confidently, but all the time my confidence was draining away, and I was less and less sure of what I was doing there. Were these the people I wanted to become? When the questions moved increasingly into areas of government policy—the recent Green paper on education, the government's position on Northern Ireland—I became more and more vague and unsure. The feeling I had, sitting in that upstairs room in the heart of the city where I was born, was one of displacement. The feeling overlapped with my experience of the exam. The gentlemen grew quieter, their questions turned away from the heavy waters of policy, and for the rest of the interview we plain-sailed over my hobbies and education. But already I knew that I had failed the test. I was not going to become a third secretary in the Department of Foreign Affairs; unlike my father, I was not going to become a civil servant of any kind.

Coming out into O'Connell Street, having received a cool good-bye from the three public servants, I remember being bitterly disappointed and wondering how I was going to tell Chris back in New York. How could I explain it? Since I had done so well in the exam, we had spent a month or so dreaming of a new life. Now, although I had not yet been informed that I had not been accepted, I knew those dreams were over. I knew that they had been false.

I have been thinking of all this again now in Kiltumper, how a life that might have gone one way took another turn. What has taken me this long to understand is exactly why I wished so dearly at the time to come home from America to enter the diplomatic service. What was it that disappointed me about the man in the consulate, and then about the three men on the interview board? What had I expected? What was it that, there in New York, I was so desperately craving?

The more I think about it now, almost ten years into a life in a rural village in Clare, the more I realize that one of my life's obsessions has been the search for a sense of belonging. Somehow, growing up in Dublin, I had lost that, had been unable to feel that the sprawling red-brick suburbia was in any way *my place*. I hadn't lived within an Irish community in America. What I had hoped to find—however unrealistically—on the day I walked into the consulate on Fifth Avenue was the beginnings of a sense of coming within a community. And it was my feeling of being outside that community, and not the failing at the interview, that so bothered me in the weeks afterwards. I truly did *not* belong there.

This week again I thought of that. Chris had gone to the Burren Painting School in Lisdoonvarna, and Deirdre, Joseph and I, as usual, dropped in on our neighbors. It was raining, and not having been in Upper Kiltumper for a while, we took the road up to the Dooleys'. Breda Dooley is Mary Breen's sister. She is married to Michael, a silver-haired and blue-eyed farmer of sixty. He's a striking, handsome man, who keeps his small farm like a well-run machine. He's fit and so at ease in his life in the outdoors that you cannot imagine him anywhere else. Neither Michael nor Breda drives a car, and at different times they can be seen going to or from the village on their bicycles; Michael, capless, and slightly askew on his seat, and Breda with her red woolen hat and scarf, solid as the bike. They have three grown daughters, two of whom have left home. One of them, Maura, married to a Corofin man, is a teacher in the Bronx. The Dooleys' house was quiet that rainy afternoon. Michael was out about the townland somewhere, and as we came up to the house Breda came out to greet us.

"Hello, Niall and Deirdre and Joseph, ye're welcome, ye're welcome, come in." She shook our hands strongly and smiled and brought the little posse of us into the main room, where it turned out Mary Breen was already sitting by the fire. She had come up across the fields to pass the wet afternoon with her sister.

"Well, what's the news below?" said Breda brightly. "How are ye all? How's Crissie? Have you heard from her?"

Breda's house was less than half a mile from ours, but on a drizzling day we could bring one another company and small fragments of news that would keep the weather away. Though her children were grown up, Breda still managed to pull out a box of small toys for Deirdre and Joseph; they were old and had passed through many hands but were none the less for that, and as we chatted the children played with them before the open fire where the kettle hung hissing. Talking and listening, keeping the conversation going, Breda came and went from her back kitchen. We talked about John Joe Russell, a neighbor and a bachelor, a fine musician who had played tin whistle at parties down at our house. He had gone to hospital in Dublin (Would I be going up again soon, and maybe Michael'd have the lift with me?), and, Breda told me, he'd brought his tin whistle with him, but what with the radiation treatments on his throat, he shouldn't really be playing. "What harm, but didn't a young nurse see it there," said Breda, "and ask him to play, and wasn't there a little bunch of them around him after a while. Sure he loved that, Niall."

"Of course he did."

"He has no relatives in Dublin or he'd be let out at weekends and back in then for the treatments. Michael was up to him last week all right. He went up in Cleary's lorry. That's a handy way up, only you have to go very early—four o'clock, I think it was, Michael cycled down, and ye're above in Dublin at half past eight."

Breda returned from the back kitchen and laid the table for

tea. As usual she didn't really ask, and though she said she had nothing much to offer us, only a few potato cakes from the griddle on the fire and a few scones with jam, it was as always wonderful, good food, made all the more hearty by the simple generosity with which Breda offered it. And as the talk went on about John Joe, and his few cattle that Michael was looking after, and how long he'd be away out of the townland, I was struck by how completely cared for he was, how he was in the thoughts and talk of his neighbors. That said more to me about community than anything else. Sitting there drinking the tea and eating the scones, I had no doubt in my mind that if I was the one gone to Dublin for radiation therapy there would be neighbors here talking in the same way of my welfare and thinking perhaps of a lorry trip to Dublin to visit me. There, at the Dooleys' in the drizzling afternoon, was the thing I had been looking for all my adult life, a sense of being within a community, however small; being knit into the fabric of a townland, belonging there despite being an outsider in so many ways.

"Having a nice holiday?" asks a man in Lisdoonvarna painting his house in between the cold raindrops.

I look at him and say sweetly, "I'm *not* on holiday."

Well, I am sort of on holiday, but not in the way he meant.

No, I am in Lisdoonvarna to sketch and paint. I am on holiday from Kilmihil, transplanted from one side of Clare to the other.

But I say "I'm not on holiday" to him for the umpteenth time, aware, as always, that as I haven't lost my American accent completely the questioner expects, presumes, that I will continue the conversation. So I enlighten him—a tiny bit.

"I live here. In West Clare, in Kilmihil. But I am from New York."

He nods as if he knew it all along. "That's a long way off."

He looks sideways at me, trying to guess rather than ask what would bring a Yank like me to West Clare. "How d'ye like it?" He is not going to *ask* me what I'm doing here. He's hoping that I will tell him, be open and talkative, like he expects Americans to be.

To placate him I say, "I like it fine, except for the weather." (I just can't seem to keep quiet about that.) I think he can't possibly argue or come back with a smarter remark because the weather is truly bad this summer. I mean, look at him. It's July and he has his overcoat on and he's trying to paint his house in the rain.

He eyes me again, sideways, with that semi-vacant look that reveals nothing but says everything to me because I have seen it so many times before. I am getting used to it, this nearly imperceptible way Irish countrymen have of communicating without talking. It's part of conversation. It's body language. It's like the empty half-beat measured out before the steps in the set dance begin. What can he say? Will it take him long? Will he say anything at all? Yes, he does.

He says, "At least you're not living on the banks of the ol' Mississippi, *girl*. No floods here. Count your blessings."

"I love you to bits!" I said to Joseph before I left home.

And he said, "I'm not Two Bits, I'm Joseph!"

It seems that I travel with my children even when they aren't with me. They seem as much a part of me, physically, now, as the clothes I put on in the morning or the purse I grab on my way to the shops. They are part of the way I think and feel, too. This morning when I reached into my cosmetic bag, here in Lisdoonvarna at the Burren Painting School, I found Joseph's red wooden toy, the one that squeaks when the little round capped head is pushed down. And Deirdre is with me, too, in the little pocket on the sleeve of my rain jacket, where I find her miniature book just one-inch square and her itty-bitty pencil. As I begin this week of sketching and painting it is a comfort to find them with me, although I can't shake off the feeling that they are reminders that I should be with them now and not here. But Niall has encouraged me and *insisted* that I come, because it has been a long time since I've painted—two years, since Joseph came into our lives. It's time to get started again.

Still, I am their mother first, no matter what I am doing or where I am. And like other mothers without help the world over, I wash their clothes, buy their groceries, cook their meals, clean their rooms, and if there is time, I play with them. Too often it feels like the business of life robs us of the living of it.

✦ TWELVE ✦

The results of this year's Tidy Towns Competition have been announced. The village scored 124 points, three *less* than the previous year. Considering that many of the houses in the village had been painted, a new stone wall built before the church, the church garden planted, two trees set in the little traffic islands at the end of the village, and a litter league operated all summer by the children to keep the streets clean, this is bad news indeed. But perhaps only to the handful of people who have been involved. For a day or two after the results were printed in the paper there was still some talk of its being a misprint; it surely wasn't possible that we had actually gone *backwards?* But soon the official report arrived and confirmed the result. Perhaps the inspectors had come too early in the season before any of the work had been carried out? After all, some improvements had not been implemented until July and the flower tubs were planted late. Whatever the reasons, the news was a blow. I began to feel the old difficulty of life in a rural place: how slow change is. The will and efforts of a handful of people do not necessarily bring about much improvement. What we needed was to involve the entire community, but by and large the community was made up of outlying farms and cottages in townlands miles from the village.

The pattern was repeating itself. I felt everything was impossible, the frustrations of doing anything were simply too great, it was best to do nothing. In such moods the cottage and the garden become our isolated kingdom. Here it is possible to make and do everything right. We work on, digging, moving plants, and planning like the master builders of some intricate dream. But always, after a time, my feelings rebound and I realize that we cannot simply live here without trying in some way to give back to the community. Whatever we can do, it behooves us to do, whether in the drama group or the school or elsewhere. The survival of the west of Ireland as a place of community and caring depends not on governments but on people's willingness to take on the difficult challenge of keeping the place alive.

A week after the news of the Tidy Towns result I began to talk to Chris out in the garden of what could be done for next year, how money could be raised, what planting plan could be drawn up. As the year was turning into autumn I imagined the same feelings were running through small villages in many rural corners of the country.

Two days later I received a letter from a county councillor in response to the complaint I had finally sent in about the condition of the Kiltumper road. The letter read, "It is going to receive priority on the next rota." We could expect that one mile of the road would be resurfaced in the new year. I was delighted. Here it was, proof that if you kept trying you did get things done, that the wheels of change did turn if you kept your shoulder against them long enough. I came up to Chris waving the letter.

"Good news about the road!" I said.

"What is it?" She put her pitchfork in the ground and reached out a muddied hand to take the letter.

"Next year! A mile is going to be resurfaced."

She looked up from reading the short letter and shook her head.

"What's wrong? It says we'll have priority on the next rota."

"Yes," she said. "That means we're to go through the winter again with it like this. And"—she pulled the fork from a clump of muck—"we had the same letter a year ago. *Top* priority."

The pitchfork hit the ground with a dull thump.

A Japanese Garden in Kilmihil? Why not?

I had approached the county arts officer, Eugene Crimmins, with a proposal to paint murals on the outdoor shelters in the yards of the four national schools in the parish. He said he'd think about it. Six months later, he phoned me to ask if I had anything else in mind for a community arts project. The wackier the better, he said. That's what got funded these days.

So I thought about it and got back to him with two ideas: a contemplative Japanese-style gravel garden and a sculpture garden, one for the area called the "new houses," which has two upward-sloping plots of land, one on either side of the road into it, and the other for the blessed well in the forest behind the house. He liked the idea of a Japanese garden, so we decided to approach the sixteen or so houses in the council estate in Kilmihil. The council estate is an area of Kilmihil village that after twenty-one years still hasn't completely settled in for various reasons. The residents have always been viewed, unfairly, as outsiders. Whether they knew it or not, I had always felt a certain affinity with them, being an outsider myself.

The project was meant to be between a community of mostly over- twenty-fives and an artist, coming together in the name of community art. Eugene and I decided that if I could involve the estate residents in this project it would be great for them and great for the village. So, with Father Malone, I knocked at every door and told everyone about my plan to make a gravel garden on the eyesore patch of ground that nobody seems to care for. I explained that the county arts officer and the council were prepared to put about £600 into the project if I could get the people to help me make it. I needed volunteers. They wouldn't be paid. What did they think? I was a bit skeptical myself but as I was received warmly at every house, I was encouraged.

When I told Eugene that we had an overwhelmingly enthusiastic response, he went ahead and deposited the funding for the project into the bank. The Kilmihil Moving Landscape Project! What a title! It'll be the first of its kind in West Clare when we're finished. As Niall says, "Chris, here you go again!"

Among our summer visitors was a woman with the un-Irish-sounding name of Mary Beth Schillachi from San Francisco. She had come up, she explained, from Glenbeigh in Kerry where she had a house, and where she visited most summers. Something in the books we had written had touched a deep chord in her, a feeling for the quality of rural Irish life, and as it turned out, an echo that went back to her childhood. Her maiden name was O'Riardain and for years her father had lived in Glenbeigh. Her connections to the rural west were even stronger than ours.

Sitting in our kitchen in Kiltumper, Mary Beth was a

reminder of the constant flow and ebb of Irish people, rippling outwards from every parish in the country. Before she left that day, she invited us as a family to take her house in Glenbeigh for a week's holiday in August. And we gratefully accepted.

So at the close of the drowned summer, we drove down into Kerry again, heading into the shadow of the mountains. We had been to Glenbeigh before and knew it as a pretty holiday village under a wooded hillside on the bend of the road from Killorglin to Cahirceveen, a stopping place in the days when horses and carriages had clopped along the scenic Ring of Kerry. At Mrs. Brennan's we stopped for the key, not a little struck by the circuitousness of collecting keys to a Kerry house we had never seen, to which we had been invited because of the written words about a life in Kiltumper read in San Francisco. I imagined, as I went in for the keys, that Mrs. Brennan might want to give us a good look over, or that she was shaking her head at the idea of Mary Beth's handing over the place to us. I need not have worried.

"Will ye follow me so?" said Mrs. Brennan, going with a brisk and friendly look to her car. "It's the high road."

Beyond Glenbeigh itself, we crossed over the river on the one-car-width bridge, under the shadow of the wooded hillside, and out down to the fabulous three-mile beach at Rossbeigh. We followed Mrs. Brennan up the steep edge of the hillside, the children giggling as we rose above the spectacular outstretched finger of sand, driving on the very edge of the peninsula that looked across the bay to Inch.

Kerry is magical, and the years of visiting and revisiting have not dulled that feeling. It is a feeling made of the landscape, of sea and mountain, wildness, rock, and solitariness. The house perched on the edge of one mountain facing another with the sea in between. We felt almost as soon as we arrived that we had moved *within* a landscape and that the long bright days of a hundred weathers held us there, no different from the goats on the hills or the blooming heather—Chris climbing the mountain at the back of the house with her sketchpad, sitting alone high up in the brilliant light of the evening, the sheep and goats nosing around her; me walking down the steep hill to the bend where suddenly the full arc of the bay swung out into the distance: moments within the landscape.

The children, too, seemed infected with this sense of being inside and outside at the same time. In the first days of the holiday as we went on walks into the mountains or down the dropping road to the sand, we did not feel that we were simply visitors, handling or browsing the countryside, snapping it for picturesque souvenirs. For our life in Kiltumper has changed how we see the rest of the country, and the landscape is more beautiful for being, to us now, a living tapestry.

Coming to Kerry from Clare for a week in another person's house isn't exactly everyone's idea of a vacation but it's the most we can do right now. The children love it. Joseph keeps calling it his holiday house. And Deirdre, who sometimes tires of living in the cottage, likes the newness of everything—the level and carpeted floors, closets, dimmer lights and bedside tables with lamps. The hallway is a novelty to them and they play hide and seek behind the four bedroom doors. It's an ordinary bungalow, really, but warm and clean and cozy, with a view that is brilliant.

I was sketching the mountain before us from the kitchen table and the children were watching the family of goats that cruise down the hillside, up the road, and onto the lawn every morning.

"Oh quick, Mammy, paint that black goat there. Please, please," begged Deirdre.

"All right, all right," I said, wanting to oblige her, and opened the field sketchbox of watercolors that Niall had given me in anticipation of this week. Deirdre was thrilled and yelled out the window, "Stop moving, goat, so Mammy can paint you!" And Joseph shouted, too: "Stop moving, goat, will you!"

The children did not really mind as I headed off with my sketchpad in the drizzle or fog or sunshine. Eithna, our young friend and neighbor, had come with us for the first couple of days to help mind the children so I could spend time sketching.

When the tide is out, the beach extends nearly half a mile. Horses gallop along the beach, walkers along the Kerry Way backpack by the house at all hours, and a one-seater, bicycle-wheeled aircraft contraption keeps circling our heads and uses the beach for takeoffs and landings. The children love this especially. Ice-cream cones and chips and baby crabs and hundreds of tiny seashells embellish our time here.

Low round white rolling clouds like waves float above the Dingle Peninsula for three days of sunshine. I can only seem to sketch the atmosphere of fleeting colors and disappearing shapes as the black shadows move quickly across the mauvey mountains that come sharply down to the sand dunes and coarse grass.

Chris and I took an afternoon drive westward along the Ring of Kerry, one of the most celebrated journeys in Ireland, but one that for Chris is just a little too touristy. She gets dismayed sometimes at what the Irish think the Americans want. The tour bus companies follow an agreed route counterclockwise, and in an hour's drive in August we passed or were passed by thirty-five coaches from various places in Europe, all snaking their way along that spectacular panoply of mountain and seascape.

It was late afternoon by the time we arrived in the holiday resort of Waterville, one of those seaside towns in which, drenched in a blue light with white waves crashing, it seems forever summer, forever the place of ice-cream cones and walks along the seafront. Everything about the town was bright and holidaylike.

Chris, as usual, did not want to drive back the way she had come—an American characteristic, I thought—but already we were late for getting back to Eithna and the children. We were also more or less halfway around the ring. Outside Waterville we pulled over and looked at the map.

"There's a road," said Chris, "here, look. We can cut back

through the mountains. It looks like we take the first left."
We drove on.

"Here, this is the first left. Right here," I said.

"Are you sure?"

"I didn't see any other, did you?"

"I guess not," Chris said.

We were just past the sign for the town itself. "This *is* the
first left," I said. So to avoid returning along the same way
we had come, and to try and cut back across the mountains,
we turned off the main road outside Waterville. Within
minutes we had left the seaside town behind us. It was a quiet
country road, off the Ring and away from the tour buses.
There were tall trees and a leafy shade, and nobody about. It
was like stepping through one of those two-way mirrors and
arriving at the inner life of the country that only we could
see.

As we drove on, still less than a mile off the main road, we
came upon a large estate with stone piers and tarmac driveway. On the wall was the sign CLUB MED. In there, behind the
high wall and the lush shrubbery and trees, you could hear
the ping of tennis balls and the whack of golfers driving off
into the tall green netting of this, the newest Club Med in
Europe, four hundred miles from the Mediterranean. Here,
in the secluded corner of the West Kerry peninsula, was a
holiday camp for those who literally wanted to get away from
it *all*. Everything you wanted, ran the ads, was right there.
The Waterville Club Med was run exactly the same way as
those in the south of France or in Switzerland or Italy. It was
active and sporty. But as we drove past the walls we couldn't
help feeling how bizarre it was there, almost hidden in rural
Ireland: a holiday place that borrowed the mood and atmo-

sphere, the beauty of the mountains and the wildness in the air, while keeping its modern, pampered population within the camp.

We had driven twenty minutes further on a narrow road of remarkable scenic beauty, all outcroppings of rock and the salmon and trout lakes of Currane and Capall, when Chris began to wonder if I had in fact taken the wrong road home. It seemed to wind on along the lakeside forever, so utterly untravelled and still and serene that the low flight of a curlew across the sky-lake was like the breaking of a mirror held to the afternoon. Miles out in this beautiful valley, we at last came upon an athletic-looking middle-aged woman walking her bicycle. I pulled the car over.

"Excuse me, can you tell me if this road comes out the other side of the mountain?"

She looked at us blankly and I repeated the question. But even before I had finished speaking she was shaking her head and pointing back along the road toward Waterville. "Club Med," she said, and smiled, unable to say anything else in English.

We smiled back and drove on. And I thought to myself that we were perhaps the only Irish people who had spoken to her on her entire holiday. Yet here she was in West Kerry, cycling through the lakeside paradise, enjoying her visit to "Ireland," unable to speak to or to make contact with any Irish people.

Fifteen minutes later, Chris was certain I had taken the wrong road. "This, sweetheart, is the road that leads to somewhere called Craiques," she said. "It doesn't come out. It's a dead end."

There were no houses now anywhere along the valley

road, only a smaller cooler-looking lake and a rising mountainside in the shade of the sun. It was lovely and lonely. We drove on in a hush, realizing that we were completely lost. And then, after an empty stretch in the road no different from any other, there was suddenly a building. It was an old national schoolhouse built in the same style and of about the same age as Clonigulane. There was smoke coming from the school chimney and outside a sign that said, MUSIEM, IONAD OIDHREACHTA, Museum and Heritage Center, Open 2.00–6.00.

We could hardly believe it. Here was the local schoolhouse turned heritage center. There had been no signs for it anywhere along the road. It was simply there, waiting, part of the landscape.

As much to ask our way as to pay a visit, we went up to the schoolhouse door. I put my thumb on the old latch and from inside at the same moment it was lifted and the door opened.

An elderly woman in a thick skirt and woolen shawl smiled and greeted us in Irish. She stood to one side and gestured us into the schoolroom, where another woman of the same age was sitting before the burning turf fire. She, too, stood up to welcome us, and in that way Irish speakers seem to have developed of sounding their first words in the language to visitors with a wavering and testing caution, she spoke a little phrase in which I caught the words "*failte*" and "Teach Bhride."

"You're our first visitors today," said the woman who had opened the door, smiling warmly at us standing there in the middle of the old schoolroom at five in the afternoon. "Here, you can sign here," said her companion happily, indicating a visitors' book.

I looked around us in amazement. The schoolroom glistened: the high ceiling boards painted yellow, the walls blue, school desks with porcelain inkwells, the old blackboard with a handful of chalks at the base of it awaiting the return of the master. Everything had been restored. The turf in the fire was *slean*-cut, and burning as if to warm the master's backside while he gazed down over the lowered heads. Along the wall were a series of glass cases and as one of the ladies led Chris around them, so her companion took me along the cases on the other side.

"These are the original rollbooks of the school," she said with a gentle pride. "Of course we had to have them rebound, but you can read the names, see." She offered one to me by a high window that looked down to the empty road.

The names were written in Irish in a palely mixed ink that had run ever so slightly under the press of blotting paper eighty years earlier. You could almost hear the scraping of the nib.

"We have a rollbook going back to the hedge school master," she said, leading me ever deeper into the past. Everything of the life of the schoolhouse had been found, cleaned, restored, and put back in its place. People had sent things back from America, from Australia; the fragments of this room's life had now been lovingly reassembled. Here were the schoolbooks the pupils had studied a hundred years earlier, a young girl's composition on Christmas, a copy of the multiplication tables. If you held the pages you could smell the classroom and slip easily through the doors of time, arriving like a *cigire*, a visiting inspector, to hear the voices of boys and girls chanting, "one-and-one-is-two, one-and-two-is-three."

The schoolhouse was a two-room building and the second room had been converted into a kind of museum, filled with the artifacts and work implements of the people of the region. In a little leaflet the world of work was cleanly divided. There was *Obair na mBan*, Women's Work, and *Obair na bhFear*, Men's Work. Under Women's Work it read: "Chiefly to do with Feeding and Clothing," and there to one side of the little backroom was an assortment of quern stones for grinding oats and corn, dough trays, basting ovens and griddles for the open hearth. There were butter churns and a spinning wheel and on the wall examples of floor rugs, quilts, lace and crochet work. The industry of the women seemed imprinted in the bowls and jugs and dishes, in the million potatoes and loaves of brown bread that had crossed the surfaces of these pots and pans before they had landed here in the schoolroom in the valley of Glenmore.

It was the same for the tools of the men—the awl and hammer; the leather, wax, and thread of the vanished shoemaker; the tailor's goose, the wooden sleeve and leg he used for pressing in the making of clothes that had all since gone to dust. There were the tools of the thatcher and the plain farmer, and a whole graveyard of shovels and spades and pikes and reaping hooks that had slashed and cleared and dug the drains and drills of the place about the schoolhouse.

As the two gentle elderly ladies brought us around the room and back again to the fireplace, it was impossible not to be subdued by their grace and pride. The four of us stood in a little cluster in front of the fire. On the wall we had passed coming in was a hand-drawn chart of the world with arrows going out from the Glenmore Valley in County Kerry.

"We traced the past pupils," said the lady in the shawl. "You see all the places they went to."

We had not the heart to say that we were in a hurry, or that we had simply been lost and come in for directions. From the map we could see we had to turn back. And yet, in the fifteen minutes or so that we spent with Breda O'Connell and her sister Maire O'Shea, it seemed as if we had arrived at the place we had set out for.

It was difficult to walk away, to leave those two women in seats by the fire, waiting for visitors. As we stood there by the map of the world with the arrows denoting the travels of the former students, into the quietness came the sound of a car approaching. One of the women lifted an eyebrow. Car doors banged and footsteps came up the gravel and the door was unlatched as another elderly woman arrived with her family.

"More visitors," I said.

"Oh no," said Mrs. O'Connell, after she had finished greeting all the newcomers. "This is our other sister. She's come to take over for the next while."

We left them in the classroom, exchanging news in Irish, changing the guard.

The brilliant light of the afternoon had softened, and the road and the roadside were burnished with a golden air as we, the only visitors to Teach Bhride that day, drove back along the way out of the valley. It was a route of emptiness and beauty, all the more poignant now that there are no schoolboys or schoolgirls passing these hedgerows, only the occasional lost cyclist from Club Med or wanderers like us. Chris felt that we had been cast under a Brigadoon-like spell and asked me to read to her the poem on the front of the little leaflet from the museum:

"Tir na loch, tir na mbeann
Tir na gcnoc, tir na nglean
Riocht gheal, alainn, aerach, draiochtach,
Aoibhinn tir na nOg."

"Land of lakes and peaks,
Land of hills and glens,
Bright kingdom, fair, bewitching.
Pleasant land of youth."

Mackerel and cucumbers for tea.

Jim came down today with a *Clematis montana* and three cucumbers from his tunnel. I keep telling Niall that we have to get one of those soon. There are a lot of vegetables that don't exactly require sun so much as light. And light we have plenty of here in Ireland in summertime. Sun, well, sometimes that, too.

"Here, Crissie," said Jim as he handed me his homegrown cucumbers. "I don't think these'll be as sharp as the ones last year. And Kay wanted you to have the clematis."

"Oh thanks, Jim," I said, genuinely delighted. "We can have the cucumbers with our tea this evening."

Jim and I have great conversations about gardening so he stayed for his usual cup of tea and chatted and then disappeared back through the archway, home to Kay.

As I was preparing the cucumbers for supper, a boy appeared through the archway just as suddenly and unexpectedly as Jim had, and I opened the glass door for him.

"Hello," I said, puzzled.

"Do ye want any mackerel?" he asked shyly.

"Sorry?" I didn't think I had heard him properly.

"We have some fresh mackerel. Would ye like any?"

"Mackerel? Ah, let me see," I said slowly. "That would be nice. Sure, I guess so. How much are they?"

"Thirty pence each," he replied.

"Okay, let's have five then." And he turned, disappeared, and came back with five shiny fresh black and blue mackerel wrapped in newspaper.

The boy was happier now. "We just caught them this evening. They're fresh from the Doonbeg River."

"That's great," I said. "Thanks very much." He took his money and left and I went back to preparing the supper. Just like that.

Everyone along the road that evening had had the same visitor and everyone along the road was having mackerel for tea. But not everyone was having fresh cucumbers as well.

✦ THIRTEEN ✦

Bad news this evening. Garry Hynes has announced that she will not be seeking to renew her contract as artistic director at the Abbey at the end of the year. This feels like a defeat, for the sense of anticipation and possibility had been so strong when she was first approached in Galway for the position. How daring it had seemed to bring this woman from the West to run one of the great establishments of the Dublin cultural scene. It seems a defeat not only on a personal level, but in some way to symbolize the misunderstood and often incompatible relationship between the two halves of this country.

For Chris and me tonight, there is real personal worry. What will happen now to my second play? For despite the fate of *The Murphy Initiative* we knew Garry was an ally up there in Dublin. Now we have no one there who is on our side. And a playwright cannot succeed unless someone will put on his plays.

We were at the ruined end of the lost summer. August drifted past in veils of mist and rain and Deirdre and I prepared our bags for school once more. I oiled the chain on my bike and checked the air in the tires. Out in the vegetable garden the potatoes were blighted badly, the stalks withering a grayish color and leaking a slithery ooze into your palm when you grasped one to pull it. Beneath the ground the potatoes themselves were small but whole, and as the children played tea party beneath the sheltering branches of an old weeping ash, Chris and I began the job of taking up the tiny white tubers, hardly enough to fill a pot. The pheasants, I hoped, had taken the bean plants. Then they had disappeared without a trace just a month or so before the sound of gunshots in the valley signaled the arrival of the Kilmihil Gun Club. ("Very few birds up around yer way this year.")

After the deluge of summer we moved into September with little hope, anticipating the closing-in nighttimes and the long winter ahead. By November it would be dark by five and the brightness of the summer evenings would have vanished into the memory of another disappointing time. There wasn't a man or woman in the parish who, after three minutes of conversation, didn't say: Wasn't it a terrible year? Disappointment was a shared emotion this season, and in a way it served to bring people together, to bind the farmers and their families up and down the western coastline who shared a fate of endurance. Even talking about it, naming the wet months, was a kind of solidarity, a way of coming through.

"But won't it make the winter very long," a man in a brown jacket said to me, when I picked him up in the car as he was walking home soaking wet.

"It will."

"Oh it will, very long. That's right. But you never know but that it might clear yet."

This had been the prayer of June, of July, and August— that it might clear yet, an annual aspiration as the farmer looked out across the fields from beneath a cap and watched the animals mucking the places that should have been hard and dry. Down the road Michael had been worried. The turf was getting no chance; there were brown slippery carpets of the stuff spread everywhere, waiting for a drying wind. By August the whole of the year's turf harvest hung in the balance, and for many families who live on the constant edge of survival it began to look like the leanest winter. But still the weather remained broken. I was about to put away the little plastic pool that Deirdre and Joseph like to splash in at the end of the garden.

It is impossible perhaps to catch the exact gloom of a lost Irish summer. Partly, I suppose, it has to do with the failure of promise, the fabulous stretch that comes in May, and the anticipation of the undying light of midsummer when you can walk through the garden nearly at midnight and see the flower colors still gleaming. It is the loss of the Atlantic in full summer, that tumbling blueness and surf when the power of the ocean seems to crash, paradoxically, with gentleness and ease. Partly it is the feeling that we have missed our one chance for another whole year. We knew the drizzle and mist of this cold summer could now stretch on right into December.

We began to prepare for nothing else, like people about to set out early on a long journey into winter. We had been through a summer like this one before when we first arrived in Kiltumper. But that did nothing to soften the disappointment. Chris especially missed the sense of season, the fullness of summer in the garden.

"Our carrots are still not moving," she reported from the garden in September. "The beans are *still* waiting for the summer."

We had begun to surrender the garden to the weather when the change came. We awoke one morning and it was a blue October day. I cycled down to teach at the school and could feel the huge lift in everything. We had come through. The day, thin and fine and delicate as a blue wafer, hung there in the sky. There were no clouds. No wind. It was as if somebody had stolen in in the darkness and changed the scenery. Under this fabulous blue sky the fields were newly green, birds flew out like refugees, and the countryside began to breathe.

The following day was just as still and blue. And the day after and the one after that. The leaves turned on the trees and the hedgerows became high shoulders of spangled color above the roads. The fuchsias and wild woodbines were gilded. In almost ten years in the west of Ireland we had never seen autumn color, for always the snap winds and driving rain showers of the end of summer had scoured and scrubbed the trees bare. Now, about the cottage, the high old sycamores held their color like fabulous brushes dipped in the autumn hues. Across the garden and down the valley the brilliant dying of the summer color was everywhere, in bushes and small trees, startling in the melancholy and moody light of the cooler sun of October.

For a week there was no rain. And then for a second week, and a third. It was a flame season, leaf-burnished, and the country boreens of West Clare that Chris and I have come to know so well over the years were newly beautiful.

The farming community threw itself with enormous energy into the finishing of the summer tasks. This was a last chance, and there was no knowing for just how long He could hold off the rain. So, in October, families went to the bog to try at last to bring home the fuel for another winter.

Our own turf was still on the bog. It had dried and been footed months earlier with Joe and Regis and the girls, and I had second-footed it a month later. But the wetness of the summer had made puddles on the soft places, and the turf had sat on, soaking up again from beneath what the winds had taken from it. The way in to the turf bank itself, a tractor track that at one point passed narrowly between some sally bushes, had become waterlogged; even in the dry days it was still spongy and gurgling underfoot. We could not be sure that a tractor and trailer loaded with turf wouldn't sink in and be stuck. In the meantime Michael Downes told me at least to bag the turf, to save it against more rain. Two days later Paul O'Shea from down the road, hearing that I was looking for big plastic fertilizer bags, dropped off fifty at the house. He had another fifty below for me when I wanted them, he said.

I went up the hill fields in the blue afternoons carrying the bags, leaving Nancy, the mare, and Nellie, the donkey, trotting over to the stone-wall bounds to watch me. As I took the sods and put them into the bags, clearing off the turf bank until it was bare once again, I missed only the unique satisfaction there is in bringing the turf home. I had to leave it there in a fat bright cluster of plastic in the midst of the great brown bogland.

"Well," I told Chris when I got home, "at least it's bagged, and if it does start raining again it'll be protected."

"But how'll we get it home?"

"I'm not sure."

"Everyone's so busy with their own right now."

"I know. But Mary still has turf up on the bog there, and maybe I can ask Michael Donnellan to . . ."

"But he has his own, too, as well as Mary's."

It was left at that. Without a tractor of our own we couldn't be sure of how or when or by whom the turf would be brought home, and I decided to put my faith in the weather's holding until everyone had their own tasks done and we might ask someone to bring down the bags.

The flame season continued and October became the driest month of the year. Deirdre settled back to school and was allowed to wear the bright summer dresses that had never seen August. One afternoon toward the end of the month Chris drove down to the village with the children to collect me from school. (My bicycle was being repaired by young Francie Downes—"the boy for bikes, Niall.") As we drove home, Deirdre pointed out to Joseph the hill fields of the farm that we could see in the distance.

"Daddy," she said, "there's a tractor in our field."

"No, no," I said without looking. "That must be in Coughlan's; there's no tractor in our fields."

"Yes, there is, Daddy, look!"

We drove in by the cabins and all went up to the back gate of the big meadow to take a look. And there it was—a tractor coming down across the hill fields of Tumper pulling a trailer piled high with plastic fertilizer bags filled with turf. It was Michael Donnellan with Joeso, who was crouched over, standing in the tractor cab beside him.

"Is it our turf, Niall?"

"Maybe it's Mary's. He wouldn't have gone up and loaded all those bags without calling in and asking me to help. But maybe he'll go up for ours later this evening."

I had hardly finished speaking when the tractor turned right at the end of the narrow road up to the Melicans' and came roaring along towards the cottage.

"It's coming to us, Daddy," shouted Deirdre.

"Coming to us!" mimicked Joseph, taking a little jump in his Wellies. "Coming to us," he said again with delight, for all the world as if it were Santa Claus on his sleigh and not the bright red tractor and trailer of turf bags that came through the gateway a moment later.

With a broad smile, his blue eyes bright under his woolen hat, Michael Donnellan gave a wave at us as he pulled in and reversed the trailer to the edge of the haybarn. He swung open the door and took a look back to see just where he was going to tip it.

"Cool evening, Niall," he said with a grin.

"Why didn't you tell me you were going up for them, Michael?"

"Ah sure," he smiled.

"I would have gone up and loaded them for you."

"I know, sure, but. Open that pin there, Joeso. I was

getting down some for Mary and I thought I'd fit yours then, you see. It can be drying away in there."

We stood there and watched as he and Joeso tipped out the turf into the haybarn. I just didn't know how to thank him. Chris and I both felt very grateful. But Michael simply shrugged it off. As he climbed up on top of the turf pile and emptied the bags with me we talked about Clare's chances in football this year. I didn't know then, nor did Michael mention, that the bringing home of our bags had taken him some time, that his tractor had gotten stuck coming out from the bank, and that Mary, up there with him, had had to go way off across the bog to find Michael Downes and ask for his help, that he had left what he was doing and had gone to tow Michael Donnellan out of trouble, all to bring home our turf that afternoon in October.

Even with my tennis elbow still inflamed because of too much gardening, not to mention just plain stress, I am determined to have a stack of turf this year. The neatness and orderliness of it appeals to me—order from chaos—and I don't want to let another winter go by with a mountain of turf just tossed there in the haybarn, messy and unkempt. I have rebuilt the stone walls in a couple of places so I should be able to figure out how to make a reek of turf, I said to Niall.

I figured it out all right: You just put one sod on top of another, side by side, and Bob's your uncle. But what I didn't figure out was that it was going to take me three days! I tried to do it in one. It's not like it requires the skill of a turf cutter, I know, but it does take effort, concentration, and focus, and the rhythm of moving and placing hundreds of sods of turf became a kind of meditation. But oh my aching elbows. Serves me right. Will I ever learn to pace myself?

Sweaters thrown on the ground were the goalposts. The goal was made above the curb on the thin strip of grass between the road and the footpath. If there was a tree, all the better; if not, you took off your sweater and threw it down, trotting out into the road among the others for the goalie to kick out the ball and get the game started. Three-and-in was the name of the game; you put three goals past the goalkeeper and you became the next one yourself. For in the Dublin suburb where I grew up, it went without saying that the game every schoolboy dreamed of, the game whose players you memorized and even became in imagination as you raced about out there on the road in the dying light after school, was soccer. We paused for the passing cars coming round the bend, holding the ball underfoot and looking about for new routes to the goal before the moment passed and the game resumed with somebody dribbling the ball, head down, arms balancing, even doing a commentary and calling a famous name as he released a shot. Goalkeepers dived on the strip of grass shouting "Save!" even as they threw themselves through the air.

That soccer was an English game, a "foreign" game, as Brother Scully at my Christian Brothers school kept reminding us, didn't matter at all. And the more he tried to convince us that it was improper to play, that it was un-Irish, unpatriotic even, to be booting a soccer ball around the schoolyard, that we should only be playing Gaelic football or hurling, the more we were attracted to it. In school teams we played Gaelic football, catching the ball and fisting and soloing under the eyes of the brothers in their black soutanes perching on the sidelines; on weekends we played for various local soccer clubs. We were aware of the division even as we were sure of our preference. In our minds the game of soccer was touched with fantasy, the stars of the game on the weekly BBC television broadcasts becoming posters on our bedroom walls.

There were many Irish players in the English leagues, and when the Republic of Ireland fielded its soccer team in Landsdowne Road in Dublin we took half-days from school to go and watch the very players we had seen on the television suddenly representing *us*. We attached to them the intensity of our passion for the game. They were *Irish* soccer players. We didn't mind that under the qualifying rules of nationality players born in England whose parents or grandparents had come from Ireland were entitled to play for us. We didn't care that the players wearing the green shirts might call for the ball in cockney or scouse accents, that they might not be all that familiar with the west of Clare or Connemara. They were Irish—part of the Ireland that is in the Bronx or Queens or Queensland—and wearing green shirts, year after year, the schoolboys clicked through the turnstiles to cheer them on. The team had little success in the European or World Cup competitions then, and the day after a match when we returned to school and Brother Scully swept into class with a list of those who had been marked absent without permission the previous afternoon, he always had a victorious grin.

"Your team didn't do much yesterday, O'Neill." A pause, then: "*Football* training tomorrow after school."

Brother Scully was a big ruddy-faced Mayoman who knew that "down the country" soccer was hardly a game at all. Besides, there weren't even a lot of goals in it; who could understand the attraction of it? It was the working-class game of the English as far as he was concerned and had no bearing at all on what it meant to be Irish.

"Give me any day Mick O'Connell soloing a ball from hand to foot in one fluent movement down the field," he would say, "like it was on a ribbon." And then, when one of us fumbled a solo in practice, came his dry laugh. "One fluent movement, O'Neill. It takes skill, you see, this game."

It was about the time that Chris and I arrived in Clare that this perception of division between Gaelic football and soccer began to change. The Republic of Ireland appointed an Englishman, Jack Charlton, as team manager and the team began a successful run, which was to take it to the finals of the European championships and then on to a first appearance in the World Cup Finals in Italy. In the summer of 1990, the whole country was converted to soccer fans as the games of Italia 90 were broadcast in every pub in every village in Ireland. That memorable summer the fervor of supporters grew with each game, and husbands left their wives and borrowed and mortgaged to get to Italy, to be there, to be one of "Jack's army," the travelling thousands of singing Irish supporters cheering on their team—not one of whose members played soccer in Ireland. The entire country seemed to hold its collective breath—no car moving, no person walking down the street anywhere across the island— on that warm evening when a penalty shoot-out saw Ireland go through to the quarter finals, one of the last eight teams in the world. It is almost impossible to exaggerate how the progress of that team—less than a third of them born in Ireland—seemed to unite people across the country. "Ireland, Ireland, Ireland!!" That cry thundered up from the stands as suddenly Ireland was a force in *soccer.*

That summer consolidated a change. In the school in Kilmihil when I introduced the idea of a junior soccer team to the first years and asked how many would be interested, every hand was raised. When I took them all out on the field they came with full soccer gear in the colors of their favorite English clubs, teams from places they had never been, but would cheer for and depend upon for their weekend happiness or misery. They themselves had never played a full soccer match in their lives, but rushed onto the field and after the ball with a boy's passion to succeed, to master the game.

This week the Republic of Ireland team stood one game away from qualifying for the next World Cup in America. Inone of those ironic twists of fate the final game was to be played against Northern Ireland in Belfast. If Ireland lost, it was out of the competition—England, Scotland, and Wales had already been eliminated.

Self-division, enmity, rivalry, North versus South—and

yet *all* the players on both sides played weekly for English teams. Now the Northern team stood under the Union Jack and sang "God Save the Queen," and the team from the Republic stood under the tricolor.

The troubles in Belfast exploded at the same time. Following a series of talks between John Hume of the Socialist Democratic Labor Party and Gerry Adams of Sinn Féin, the Republican Party, there had developed a real feeling throughout Ireland that perhaps the violence and division of twenty-five years in Ulster was going to come to an end. John Hume, a respected Ulster politician, announced that his talks offered the best hope for peace since the Seventies. So it began to seem. Then, within two weeks, a series of bombings and reprisal shootings ripped through the province, and men, women, and children on both sides of the conflict were brutally murdered. The evening news spoke of Ulster in the grip of fear, of people afraid to go outside, to answer knocks at the door, of no taxis after six o'clock. It was the worst fortnight in decades: Gunmen burst into a public house and opened fire indiscriminately; a man opened the door to be shot dead before his young daughter. Hope seemed lost.

For the safety of the players from the Republic a decision was made that the game against Northern Ireland was to be moved from Belfast to somewhere in England, or even to Germany. And then, three days later, it was reset for Belfast once more.

So in the middle of November, a Republic of Ireland team was escorted into Belfast's Windsor Park to play Northern Ireland for the chance of going to America. The North had no chance of qualifying; their chief ambition was to stop the Republic.

When the players took the field the crowd erupted. Official policy had seen to it that tickets for the game were largely unavailable in the South and only a few hundred supporters of the Republic's team had managed to procure some and get to Belfast. They travelled without flags or banners, hiding their green shirts under heavy sweaters and standing quietly amidst the passionate hordes of Northern supporters.

Windsor Park that night was full of rage and volatile spite. Thousands of angry fists punched the night air, and as the game began so, too, did the jeering and the taunts. Over a million and a half viewers in the Republic watched their televisions that evening, making the confrontation between North and South one of the highest-rated programs in the country's history. And all of them heard the shouts ringing out around the ground when an "Irish" player touched the ball: "FENIAN BASTARDS! FENIAN BASTARDS!"

The players thumped the ball nervously through the middle of the field, never settling into the game. The team from the Republic had come through an eleven-match campaign in places as unwelcoming as Albania and Latvia, but nothing compared to the atmosphere in Windsor Park that night.

With ten minutes left in the game Northern Ireland scored. In our kitchen in Kiltumper our stomachs fell in unison with those of the whole country in one sickening thud. We were going to lose; in this, the very last game, we were going to be eliminated. We wouldn't be going to America after all, and the aunts and uncles and cousins and friends and ex-neighbors who had all been asked for spare rooms in New York next summer, all the dreams of getting to the States, of meeting up with relations, of its being like back when we were schoolboys dodging down to Landsdowne Road to cheer our team all vanished in that moment. The jeers and taunts grew wilder as the crowd danced in their places. "ENGLISH REJECTS! ENGLISH REJECTS!" rang out fiercely across the November night, and then the same song that had been sung in Landsdowne Road months before by the *Republic's* supporters, rollicking and partisan: "THERE'S ONLY ONE TEAM IN IRELAND!"

It only lasted for a few minutes, for almost at once the Republic scored an equalizer. There was stunned silence. The handful of travelling supporters from the South dared not cheer, but stood there in their places, knowing that below the border on the same island, in houses and hotels and pubs everywhere, people were singing and dancing.

The game ended in a tie. The team from the Republic had qualified for the World Cup. But they had not beaten Northern Ireland in Belfast.

The players were escorted away and taken under guard along an alternative route to the airport, to fly the short trip down to Dublin, where crowds were already gathering to meet them after midnight—as the novelist Dermot Bolger pointed out, the airport for once becoming a place of celebration for Ireland rather than a symbol of exile and emigration. But in the morning, as the players on both teams returned to their clubs in England and their supporters went back to work, it was the memory of the viciousness of the Northern fans that night that lingered.

English soccer clubs resumed playing league matches the following Saturday, and their supporters from Northern and Southern Ireland alike joined in cheering on Manchester United or Liverpool or Chelsea. Indeed, many from both sides of the border might have travelled over to see a game and walked up to a football ground side by side wearing their red scarves, companions.

Meanwhile in Belfast, London, and Dublin the peace talks continue.

Almost a year after the election, we have seen little of Dr. Bhamjee in the West. Following his decision not to resign over the changing of the status of Shannon Airport, he has seemed to lose face. It doesn't matter that he might be tirelessly devoting himself to dozens of other issues in the county, might be selflessly working for the good of us all. He is not in the media's eye. We read little about him now. Perhaps it is true of all politics, but in the West particularly where feelings of being neglected or abandoned by Dublin are never far below the surface, there seems a need for our politicians to be seen, up there, speaking out, being public. Dr. Bhamjee, after the wave of publicity caused by his election, seems to have slipped quietly off the news pages.

Then, in this evening's *Clare Champion*, he was featured on the front page in an article more reminiscent of the ones that surrounded his election. Dr. Moosajee Bhamjee, it read, had just accepted an official invitation from the Indian government to visit India. He was being invited, said the article, as a mark of his achievement in becoming the first Indian elected to the Irish government. The headline of the piece: BHAMJEE OFF TO FIND ROOTS!

Deirdre is back at Clonigulane in the first class, her third year at school, with our friend Martin Keane as principal. Joseph is too young for playgroup and stays at home with me except for two days a week when Mary Kilkenny minds him. Niall is back part-time teaching at St. Michael's. No permanent job there for him. Not yet. Although Larry wants him as a full-time teacher, the parents want him, and above all the students want him, the student-teacher ratio is still the same. There is no post for Niall. As it is, Larry anticipates that he will have to let Niall go. And then what? The dole? Niall always says, like Mr. Macawber, that something will turn up. And deep in my heart I believe him. We didn't come to Ireland, write four books and Niall's two plays, make my sketches, rebuild our house and make our garden, and adopt our joyful children only to have to return to America ten years later to look for work. Or should I say *paychecks*? Yes, because God knows there's plenty of work here. Why doesn't money grow on trees? Why can't the Irish live in Ireland?

Now it is midmorning and I'm facing the warm sun on a cool day in autumn. It feels like summer in the garden. I take my tea outside and sit. Max, our aging cat, begs me for food but settles on my lap, soaking up the sun with me. Our clutch of hens, Martin Keane's gift, are tapping on the door of their cabins, sensing the sunlight. The leaves are drifting. And I feel peaceful and reflective.

Nancy and Nellie are in the back meadow again. The big question on the farm now is: Is Nancy in foal and will she foal in April? Another April baby. It has been one of the disappointments of our farm life that I don't really have the time to keep a horse, not of Nancy's breeding. Some people think it's a waste to have her if she's not being ridden. And that's unfortunate, but Joseph and Deirdre come first these days, and Nancy will wait for us. She is happy here, and as I look at her chestnut figure grazing in the meadow with the gray donkey beside her I think to myself, isn't that enough for now? She has become part of the landscape, like the garden and the house. She belongs here.

As we move into autumn and winter I will watch Nancy like I watch the garden and I will be planning for next summer. The hens will stop laying for the winter but they will start up again. Max will want to come indoors more. And Nellie will still be hanging around, silent when she is happy.

Joseph will be three on April 1. We may have a foal by then and if it is a good foal we will breed Nancy again and get a family horse for the children. Deirdre and I will be a year older in April, too. Who knows, April might be a great month.

Sometimes I can so clearly see the blessings of my life here. But sometimes I let the weather and the isolation of our rural home distract me. Niall is happy here, the children are happy, and Deirdre loves school. I should say to myself more often: This is more than enough.

Because it is.

✦ Fourteen ✦

On Tuesday Chris received the manuscript. It was a small green copybook. On the front cover was written "DRAMA by Noel Downes" and a series of warnings: "PRIVATE" and "KEEP OUT," signalling the importance its author placed on the material. Inside the green covers were Noel Downes' first five plays. He had passed them on to Chris one day when, along with Deirdre, she had picked up the Downes children from Clonigulane.

"Would you take a look at them, Crissie?" he had asked from the back seat.

"Of course I will, Noel."

"And do you think, Crissie, Niall might take a look, too?"

"I'm sure he will."

"Good. Thanks, Crissie."

And so the collected first plays of Noel Downes, aged eleven, had arrived at the house, and an anxious author waited down the Kiltumper road for the first reviews. No matter what the plays were to be like, even before I opened the first page I was keenly struck by the aptness of it all, and not a little moved. The only plays Noel had seen were the annual productions we had mounted with the Kilmihil Drama Group; the theater to him was evenings of rough magic in our community center. But everything he had seen seemed to have struck a deep chord in his imagination. The first play was a five-page adaptation of a one-act comedy called *George* that had been produced in Kilmihil the year before. Like the original, Noel's play was set in a hospital ward, full of misunderstandings, wrong injections, and people falling out of bed. Martin Keane had told me that Noel was a skilled comic actor and mimic, and now in the plays he wrote everything verged on comedy and farce. The plays were dotted with misspellings, and sometimes the speeches didn't quite follow or were repetitive, but nothing could disguise the sheer exuberance of them, the joy that Noel had taken in writing them.

The five plays ran to twenty-three pages. The best one was called *Holy God*. I was laughing out loud when I read it beside the fire on Tuesday evening. It was set in a confessional. Francis, a young boy, has come for confession. Shortly after he begins the priest starts to fall asleep. Soon he is snoring on the other side of the grill from Francis. Not quite knowing what to do, Francis, too, settles down for a nap and to wait for the priest to wake up. End of Scene One. Scene Two begins when Francis and Father wake up with a start.

> FRANCIS: Where are we? Oh my God!
> GOD: That's my name.

The action has moved to heaven, and Francis and Father drop to their knees before God, the priest mortified at having been taken while he was asleep in the confessional. Francis, on the other hand, seems quite at ease.

> FRANCIS: Nice place you have here, Lord.
> GOD: Thank you, Francis, Mary did that. Oh,
>   here she is now.
> (Enter MARY with the groceries.)

Soon Francis, who has a tendency to strong language, has upset Mary and God, and after a sudden argument is about to be sent to hell when he wakes up with a start and becomes hysterical. The priest asks him to calm down in the confessional "for God's sake."

"God!" screams Francis, "Where? Where! He's after me, Agh! Let me out of here." Francis exits running, and the curtain closes.

Almost every day after the Tuesday when we got the plays, Noel asked Chris for any news. Chris told him that I would meet him for a chat about them on the weekend. On Thursday I picked up Deirdre at Clonigulane, and Noel got in along with Una and Colette and young Alan O'Shea.

"You read them, Niall?" said Noel.

"I did, Noel, and . . ."

"It's okay," he cut in. "I'll be back on the weekend to talk to you. All right?"

It was clear this was serious business between writers, not something to be chatted over on the way home from school. And I couldn't help but respect and admire him for his earnestness.

On Saturday afternoon I stopped in to Mary Breen's and as usual the chat was broken with mugs of strong tea and wedges of Mary's brown bread. Mary had heard all about the plays. "He's very eager waiting to talk to you about them," she said and shushed herself as a moment afterwards Noel himself came in the door.

He sat down at a corner of the table in his jeans and Wellies. In a little while his brother Karol would be looking for him to help drive the cattle over to the river for their drink, but he had seen my car outside and slipped in for our chat.

"When did you write them, Noel?" I asked him.

"I wrote two of them one night after I went to bed," he said.

"Two of them?" said Mary.

"And another one a few days later when I came in after the jobs. Do you think they're good, Niall?"

"I do, Noel. I think they're terrific."

"Are they?"

"Yes, they are. I think *Holy God* is the best."

"Yeah," he smiled, thinking about it. "That's a good one, all right."

Gently I tried to talk to him about rewriting and about staging. Mary brought us a pen and paper and I sat there while Joseph and Deirdre ate brown bread and drank tea, drawing a stage for *Holy God* as Noel took it all in.

"Oh yeah," he said, "like I can see them in my head, coming and going and that. Is that what you mean, Niall?"

"That's it, Noel. Anything you can see you put down here," I said.

We talked on until Karol appeared at the door in his boots and overalls to say the cows were on their way and for Noel to run down to head them off at the river.

"Right so. Thanks, Niall," said Noel, gathering up the fragment of paper with the stage drawn on it and running out to his work.

A few days later a second draft of *Holy God* arrived at the house. He had taken in what I had told him and developed the short play a little more. In the meantime, Martin Keane had told him that they would certainly try and stage the piece at the school in the new year. Now suddenly Noel was working towards a production. It was marvelous, and even as I sat in Kiltumper with Chris talking about it, it seemed for a moment like the most natural thing in the world. Maybe, just maybe, there would be other plays by Noel Downes. He would go on looking at the annual plays of the drama group and be inspired to write more or to act or to put on costumes and make up his own shows, and there might be others, too, out there in these country schools whom the theater and the idea and excitement of writing might reach. In some way, Chris and I might have begun something.

On a rainy night in December I drove into Ennis to meet Dr. Bhamjee. It is a year since the election, and the more I think back over the year—the profound hope for real change—the more I wonder if my expectations were not too high. What exactly were we hoping for? And had anything changed? I drove to Ennis with these questions turning over in my mind. I needed to find some way to measure the year, and there seemed no better way than to meet for the first time the man I had voted for a year earlier.

In the sparsely furnished Labor Party office in Ennis, a small woman was kneeling and laying photocopies like a carpet across the floor. She told me that Dr. Bhamjee would meet me in "his rooms," meaning his office where he practices psychiatry on the other side of town. I arrived at the old two-story building beside the Fergus River ten minutes late. The rain was pouring down and the red door with the brass nameplate, DR. MOOSAJEE BHAMJEE, was ajar. Following an arrow drawn on a piece of cardboard I walked up the bare stairs, struck by the oddity of coming to see a South African-born Indian in order to measure a life in Clare.

Dr. Bhamjee's office door was open, and as I walked in he was sitting in his coat at a desk scattered with letters.

"Oh hello," he said lightly. "Come in, come in, and sit down." He stood and shook my hand, holding an opened letter in his left hand. A short, solid man of fifty, his black hair is threaded with silver and his short sideburns are gray. His manner is quiet, and as he listens he leans his head a bit forward and raises his curling eyebrows. On this day he is wearing a suit of light gray cloth over a burgundy sweater with a blue tie. He keeps his coat on over everything, and I wonder if the Irish weather doesn't still, after thirty years, get inside his skin.

"You'll have to excuse me now for just one minute," he

says, turning back to the letter he holds, looking exactly the part of the member of the Dail facing the demands of his constituents. "But we can talk while I do this, it won't take long." He looks up at me an instant, eyebrows rising, to see if it is all right.

I can't quite reconcile the image of this man sitting in his psychiatry office in Ennis with the letters about road work and grant applications he is opening. And as if Dr. Bhamjee is reading my mind and finding it comic himself, he looks across at me—looking at him—and grins.

"How did you ever end up here?" I ask.

"Well," he begins, catching his breath as he does and letting it out midsentence, giving a broken, interrupted rhythm to his phrases. "A number of reasons. First one? First I came to Ireland in 1965 to study medicine. Better write that down." He indicates my notebook. "My father came from India. Was a small shopkeeper in South Africa. Ten of us there were, better get that right." He laughs out loud. "My mother says on the television interview I did—did you see that one?—I made it seem eleven, so, no, ten of us."

"And the small shop in South Africa?"

"That's right. My father didn't buy it. No, no, he rented it. One of my brothers is still there in the shop. Yes, he is. So, education, you see, my father understood, was a way out for us. There was no money. We were poor, very poor, but education, you see, that was the way. And there was this system there, you see, where the older one paid for the education of the younger, and then he got out and when he was qualified he paid for the next one and so on. And my elder brother got a bursary to start him off, from the community."

"The Indian community in the village?"

"That's right, and Ireland was known at that time to be very good for medicine, and the Irish College of Surgeons' entrance examination had an equivalency in South Africa, so you could get in, and then the cost of living was another reason. So then my brother was here, and he brought the next one and I came to Dublin."

"What did you think of it?"

"Damp, bleak, gray place. I was expecting America, you see? In South Africa we saw all these American films in the cinema, I was expecting high rises but no, no, it was very different. I remember my first bowl of porridge in my digs where I was staying. Horrible stuff."

"And what about the countryside? Did you get outside Dublin?"

"I expected huge, tall girls carrying buckets of water." He grins and lifts his eyebrows to the ceiling. "My brother, you see, said see *The Quiet Man* film, and I saw it in South Africa. So then, I was expecting these girls when I went down to the West. And I was looking around and no sign, no huge girls with buckets of water. I was disappointed really." He laughs at his own innocence.

"But you met Clare, your wife?"

"In Dublin, yes, in '69. That was a thing, too. Her father had a shop in Cooraclare—near you, right? And he sent his daughter to sample city life and then she meets *me*! But the religious difference was a secondary thing with him, he had a culture block. I suppose he thought I was going to have four wives and I would discard her after a while.

"Then, I qualified and we broke off and I went back to South Africa, to put something back into the community that had sent me out. It was the way of it."

He set the letters aside and sat back in his chair with his hands behind his head.

"So '74, yes," he continues. "Clare came out. I invited her to see the apartheid system."

"That was an interesting invitation to an Irish girl!"

"She thought it was to come out to meet my family. By that time we realized it was serious between us. There was the Immorality Law, so I couldn't marry Clare, and live with her there. I had to leave. I came back to Ireland. I remember going down to Cooraclare and Clare's mother scrubbing the floors before I got there. She thought, you see, a doctor in the house. Then, 1975, we were married. Two ceremonies, one in Gardiner Street Church in Dublin and one Moslem. I always remember, there was this priest—I am not a religious man—but he wanted an affidavit from me and for me to take six Catholic lessons. Seemed to me he was treating me like a heathen, you know, negating my culture, so we got rid of him and got a different priest, a Jesuit, you see, much more liberal. Then my father-in-law, I remember, had to go home after the wedding on the six o'clock train, to the shop. Yes, and we walked out afterwards and got the bus home! The bus, yes, I think that's very good now. Had no money, you see."

"So you stayed in Dublin then?"

"No, Cork, training to be a psychiatrist."

"And driving down to Cooraclare."

"Oh yes, whenever I went home—I always call it home—the roads getting smaller, off the main road, off the main road again, and so on, they were very accepting of me in Cooraclare. I have to say that. No racism, none whatsoever. Though I didn't go to church. They'd go, I'd look after the shop. Then, next thing, 1978, I took out citizenship, though my mind was still in South Africa. I knew—marriage, mort-gage, children coming—I had to make my home here."

"You have three children now?"

"That's right. One boy. Omar is sixteen. Funny thing he said to me yesterday: Dad, you know I'm happy you didn't call me Anthony Bhamjee or something like that. The name is strong, you know. Omar. Then two daughters—Miriam, which is Irish but also like a holy name in my culture, and Rosin, with Irish spelling, which is the sound, too, of a flower in Persia. So they are our children, our two cultures. None of them were baptized at first. But Clare is a very religious woman. I wanted to wait until they were more grown up, to decide for themselves, but what is it, Holy Blessed . . ."

"Communion?"

"That's right. They felt a bit left out. And so. Omar is Moslem. More agnostic, really."

"And what about politics," I ask him. "When did that start?"

"I was always interested, you see. Part of the antiapartheid movement in Dublin, always interested in Labor, for the poor and the working class, because of my own background. Anti-Vietnam marches, all that, too. In 1984 we moved to Clare. In 1986, then, I was chairman of the Clare Divorce Action group, a very small group at that time, but you see in my practice as a psychiatrist I could see the damage inflicted by bad marriages. I remember I was very upset when the Divorce Bill was rejected.

"Then in March 1991, some of us here decided let's have a change, let's form the Fergus branch of the Labor Party here in Ennis. Labor was very weak in Clare, very weak. They had run no Labor candidate in Clare in '89, none at all, and the fellow who ran in '87 only got 500 votes. So then I was the candidate, and I remember"—he breaks off and smiles broadly—"the phone call from Dublin and a fellow saying, 'Jesus, couldn't you find a white man to go?' I thought it was very funny. You've got to take the 'slag,' the joke, in Irish society."

"So how did you enjoy canvassing the people of Clare?"

"I hadn't a clue. Never canvassed before. I was walking up to the doors on my first day with a few supporters and they were pushing me forward, saying, 'Jesus, you're the candidate, go on!' I didn't know, I had to learn how to *plumas*," he says, sounding the Irish word for a way of being ingratiating and flattering toward a deliberate end. "But I had the children's support, they knew me because I had been involved in organizing the Clare schoolboys' soccer league. 'Bhamjee, Bhamjee!' they were shouting as I was coming down the street.

"I had to go to canvass outside the church gates of Kilkee and Doonbeg. Very few people came up to me. But they listened. They didn't want to show in public they might be considering Labor; Irish are very like that, very careful. I didn't want to go to Cooraclare, because of Brendan Daly, who was then the Fianna Fail Dail member. He lives there. Clare's family were happy about that—they were afraid they might lose business in the shop! But Brendan called me, and he said, 'Jesus, you're from the village, come on and canvass.' I appreciated that, so when I was elected I asked for no victory bonfires in Cooraclare. I thought that was only right."

"Do you remember the election itself?"

"Oh yes. I was never at an election before, you see. Never. I went down to vote and somebody said, 'Bhamjee, you're doing well' so I thought I better go home and put on a suit.

Then I heard 13 percent of the rural vote was for Bhamjee. The Fianna Fail fellows were shaking their heads—'Jesus, why is he taking our votes?' They couldn't understand it, you see.

"We didn't even want to form a government, we wanted to build up a strong Left. But Labor had to go in, and, really, the expectations were too high. Of course there was the Mullaghmore issue at the start, but I think now that will go ahead, and it will be beneficial. Then Shannon. They tried to make out I was doing nothing, but I wanted to keep the needs of the county on the agenda and now look." The decision to stop flights from Shannon to the United States had been changed yet again this week, and now the airline planned to continue operating a Shannon-New York schedule.

"Then there was a lot of social legislation that wouldn't have happened so easily—the Condom Bill [allowing condoms for general sale in Ireland] and the Homosexual Bill [decriminalizing homosexuality]," Bhamjee went on, "and we also brought on the agenda of united Ireland. But the thing is this: You can't change a conservative Irish society overnight."

"And what about the West?" I ask him, managing for once to get in a question before the answer came. "How do you see it now?"

"Well, the policies of the EC are contributing to the denuding of the west. No doubt about it. But the youth want wages, the large families are gone, and the media highlights the attractions of the cities. What is bad is the women feeling isolated. This is very important, I think, the women in the rural places. We must keep trying to support the rural communities."

He pauses and looks across the desk for a paper he has written on the subject, something that links his two worlds of politics and psychiatry. "Have I been talking too much?" he asks me, raising his eyebrows, smiling, and adding, "I like talking."

The rain is still beating in against the long windows of his rooms. Two hours have passed, and I have the feeling the doctor could talk on easily like this, deep into the night. I stand up and tell him I have to get home and he immediately asks me, "What do you think of me?"

"I think when you were voted in there was a lot of hope invested in you, and that was probably unfair . . ."

"But now that you've met me, what do you think of me?" He has come over and stands beside me, his groomed hair glistening under the light. I stand easily a head above him, in height.

"What people forget is that Irish politics is all local issues, all constituency work. I don't forget that. In other countries you have Citizens' Advice Bureaus to answer questions. Here you have your TD [Dail Deputy] Clinics. Even the taoiseach [the prime minister] has to have his clinics. I am trying to do something for the people who voted for me, you see. That's all."

There is something so genuine and earnest in the man that his appeal moves me. "I think I'm glad I voted for you," I tell him, and it really seems to matter to him. He takes some boxes and hands me some to carry down the stairs to his car. He says he'll get me the video of his TV appearance and a tape of a song someone wrote about him—"Are You Right There, Bhamjee, Are you Right?"

We go down the stairs, switching off the lights behind us,

and step out into the rain. I stand with the boxes of Labor Party brochures in my arms as he loads them into the trunk of his car. The dark rain blows over both of us.

"Aren't you going to ask me if I'll run again? Everybody asks me that. I'll tell you," he says, straightening up, and looking me in the eye, "I will. I feel I'm doing something for the Jesus bloody poor, you know. I feel I'm doing something."

"You are," I say. And with that we say goodnight and drive off separately into the dark. And all the way back along the road, the road that gets narrower and narrower as it moves into the west, I feel a sense of renewal, and the same warmth and hope of a year ago.

"Is the book gone yet?" Martin Keane asks me, leaning in the car window when I go to pick up Deirdre from school.

"Tomorrow," I tell him.

"Am I in it?" says Noel Downes, climbing in the back of the car with Una and Colette and Alan O'Shea. "Am I, am I, Niall?" come the other voices from the back seat in chorus.

"I'll put you all in," I say, "if you're good."

A cheer fills the car and I drive the little band home. "The book," as all our friends and neighbors refer to it, seems as much a part of Kiltumper activity as anything else that happens here—as if it is a communal enterprise. And in a way, I suppose, it is.

Now the Tidy Towns Committee is meeting again on Monday nights in the school with new plans and new hopes—surviving the disappointments of the previous year with humor and tenacity.

We are nearing the end of another winter of rehearsal with the Kilmihil Drama Group, and our production of Dario Fo's *Trumpets and Raspberries* is booked for the festival at Doonbeg on St. Patrick's night. The county council digger is arriving soon to begin the excavations for Chris's Japanese Zen garden down in the village.

I lost my job teaching at the high school—and got it back again when a teacher went out on maternity leave. ("You have to be gentle with him, he's on maternity leave at the moment," Chris says, teasing, to Kay in the conservatory.)

We had waited anxiously to hear from the Abbey Theatre and, one Saturday morning, I was summoned to Dublin to meet with Patrick Mason, the theatre's new Artistic Director. To our relief, he told me that The Abbey was committed to my work and wanted to put on my new play.

What tomorrow will bring I cannot say, but humor and hope will keep us going, I tell Chris.

On Tuesday afternoons now, she gives free art classes to the pupils up at Clonigulane. During the summer we painted the interior of the two rooms and the cloakroom. There are number and letter friezes along the top of the walls of the Junior Room now, a giant sunflower growing up the wall, a rainbow, and a set of handprints. The cloakroom is painted sky blue with white clouds, and a day after it was opened to the children, one of the young boys smiling and sitting on the cloakroom bench told Mrs. Callinan, "I'm having my lunch in the clouds."

Such moments are the measure of what we're doing here. As are the many times when Deirdre or Joseph delights us with exuberance or freedom or simple joy out in the garden chasing among the hens, picnicking under the sycamore trees.

. . .

The spring bulbs are up. New life is everywhere. For a week or so in April the Downes children kept calling up after school to know if there was any news: "Has she foaled yet, Crissie?" Nancy's pregnancy became a mini-event in the townland. First she was a week, then two weeks past her due date. Was she pregnant at all? Michael Dooley teased Chris, "Maybe the donkey is the one going to foal!"

"She could, too, from the size of her," rejoined Michael Downes with a chuckle. Added to the interest surrounding Nancy's pregnancy was the fact that the stallion, Pride of Tomes, had died shortly after impregnating her. So the days of waiting in April passed with not a little suspense. Then one afternoon, almost a year after visiting the stallion in East Clare, Nancy began at last to show signs.

"She's dripping milk, Niall!" Una Downes shouted, racing into the kitchen and calling up to me where I was working at the typewriter underneath the skylight in the garret room. "You better come, she's foalin', Niall!"

Out in the field around the mare were gathered Chris, Deirdre, Joseph, Una and Colette, Noel and Alan O'Shea. As horses are not as common on farms anymore, none of the children had seen a foal born and they were giddy with excitement. Each of them took part in the chorus of "She's foalin'" as I joined them. Joseph, too, was taking little leaps in his Wellies with the same shout, having no clear idea of what he was saying but delighted all the same.

"She's foalin'! She's foalin'! Hurray!"

But Nancy didn't foal that afternoon. The children left and came back again in the evening to check and then went away down the road again. Mary Breen stopped me on her way up to Breda's to ask if there was any news. Everyone was waiting now.

Chris was back in the cottage looking up horse books. I went down to the village and bought a new lamp.

"Are ye new parents yet?" asked Gregory. "She could have foaled by the time you get back."

I raced home with the new lamp—no foal. Jim had arrived with a pair of powerful binoculars and a stronger lamp. He assured us it was a good night for it and went home telling us he'd be on call whenever we needed him.

Darkness at nine-thirty. I had been told horses were exceptionally private and wouldn't foal until after midnight. I made half-hourly checks, moving across the dewy stillness of the dark meadow, hearing Nancy breathe and the slow labored movement of her hooves on the hard ground. Half past eleven and she was still slowly circling around the perimeter of the meadow, followed closely by the donkey. (Did Nellie know what was happening, too?) I came in and told Chris to go to bed; it could be hours yet.

"Well, have you everything ready?"

Flashlight, binoculars—what else would I need? Rope? Towels? Boiling water? Disinfectant? A knife—a knife?? ("She could have trouble bursting the caul," Mary had told me. "You'll want to watch her, Niall, so the little foal won't strangle or suffocate, you know.")

"Yes, I think so," I said, and sat on the couch, reminded of the days when we had first brought Deirdre home and sat nervously, in terror at her every move.

At midnight there was a long animal's screeching at the

back of the house. Chris rushed from the bed downstairs. "Did you hear that?" she called ahead of herself, as I was pulling on my boots.

I rushed out into the starry night. There, just a couple of yards from the back of the house in the small paddock, Nancy was having her foal. Already its forelegs—or were they hind legs?—were poking into the world. She stood when I came and then fell sideways with a great thump onto the grass, moving the foal forward another few inches. She stood again and neighed and blew loudly, and fell again onto her side. I couldn't believe the foal could survive such battering even as I saw it arching out into the night air. Chris was at my side in her nightgown and Wellies. The children's bedroom was only a few feet away. Down road I could see the lights of Jim's car arriving.

A last heave and the foal was born—and Nellie, the donkey, went crazy! Whether from fright or jealousy, the poor donkey had taken an instant dislike to the foal and within seconds of its birth was attempting to stomp all over it. Nancy was sweating and panting, protecting her foal as it opened its lungs for its first breath of air. The donkey began braying and tramping around excitedly. She roared and snorted with a mixture of heartache and anger, maddening the mare further and creating total pandemonium there in the night field. I dragged her off to the cabin while Jim and Chris calmed the mare.

For two more hours that night, the three of us stood beneath the stars and drank mugs of tea and watched the little ordinary miracle of the mare and her foal. The moon was hidden but the night was bright and serene, and the children slept on unaware of the surprise awaiting them at breakfast, and the exciting news that Deirdre would bring to Clonigulane. It was a wonderful ending—and beginning.

Now Nancy and "Magic Star," as the children christened the foal, are grazing together in the back meadow. They have had a stream of visitors come to wish them well—including Father Malone, who, while he was here, decided to give them a blessing. Nellie is kept at a little distance, Nancy's love affair with her over for the moment.

Looking out beneath the hanging fresh leaves of the sycamores at the new life in the meadow is peaceful and satisfying, and with the children watching the foal on its tearaway runs across the field you can feel the newness and wonder of everything again. Plans are afoot for the garden, too, this year. Perhaps *this* will be the awaited long warm summer. A lift in the clouds and a sudden brightness reminds me I'm due to get the peas planted. But first I'll turn off the typewriter and go out in the car down the Kiltumper road with Chris and Deirdre and Joseph to call on the neighbors and drink a cup of tea and say, Yes, the book is done . . .

THE END